Now she was flustered.

They may have shared a very intimate moment, a gargantuan moment in her life that she would always remember, but it was over a decade ago now and it wasn't like they were friends. They'd never kept in touch. It wasn't like they had any obligation to each other, but she couldn't understand why he was talking to her in that way. "I just... We shared something, a long time ago, I'll admit, but we did share an amazing moment together, and you and Yael were so...welcoming and kind and warm, and yet now you're just..." Should she call him cold? Distant? Unapproachable? Terse?

Anthony glanced at the receptionist, who was thankfully on a call and not listening to them at all. "We are at work, and work requires us to be professionals."

"I know that. Lives are in our hands. But we can still be professionals and nice to one another."

"You don't think I'm being nice?"

Dear Reader,

I had an image in my mind for a long time of a woman in a wheelchair with no hair, wearing a nasal cannula, clearly dying, who was holding a newborn baby who was mere minutes old, and I had no idea who they were, or what they were doing, or how they had gotten to that point. I considered many storylines for them, but none of them fit, until I went on a dog walk.

Dog walks are great for writers. They are the perfect thinking time for your writing, and if you don't want thinking time, then listen to a podcast or an audiobook and refill that creative well. Plus, fresh air, exercise, obviously!

This walk in particular gave me a light-bulb moment and I suddenly knew who everyone was. I knew what they were doing and when. And how they had gotten to that point. This story was an absolute joy to write and I had so much fun, and Anthony and Julia will stay with me for a very long time.

I hope you enjoy their story!

Louisa xxx

THE SURGEON'S RELATIONSHIP RUSE

LOUISA HEATON

MEDICAL ROMANCE

Harlequin®
MEDICAL
ROMANCE

Recycling programs for this product may not exist in your area.

ISBN-13: 978-1-335-94301-9

The Surgeon's Relationship Ruse

Copyright © 2025 by Louisa Heaton

Harlequin Enterprises ULC
22 Adelaide St. West, 41st Floor
Toronto, Ontario M5H 4E3, Canada
www.Harlequin.com

Printed in U.S.A.

Louisa Heaton lives on Hayling Island, Hampshire, with her husband, four children and a small zoo. She has worked in various roles in the health industry—most recently four years as a community first responder, answering emergency calls. When not writing, Louisa enjoys other creative pursuits, including reading, quilting and patchwork—usually instead of the things she *ought* to be doing!

For Liss, Nathan, Lemoney and all the wonderful members of the Firefly Gang! Xxx

CHAPTER ONE

Ten years ago

THE FIRST SERIOUS Braxton Hicks contraction had happened at work. Practice contractions, her mid-wife had called them. The body getting ready for birth. She'd had a few tightenings before in the last few days. Nothing lasting more than a few seconds. But this felt different.

The café in which she worked, situated in the centre of the high street in a town in the Home Counties, was overrun. Customers were grabbing coffee and cake as a brief respite from their last-minute Christmas shopping. Christmas Eve was always a busy day, and Julia was carrying a tray over to table twelve. A pot of decaf breakfast tea. One cappuccino with chocolate sprinkles arranged in the shape of a snowflake. Two mince pies with brandy cream.

The first cramp hit like a bolt from the blue.

She'd gasped, surprised, then continued on as her abdomen relaxed, her gaze flicking to the large clock on the wall. Eleven minutes past twelve. It was gone as quickly as it started and she smiled at her customers as she placed their order down on the table, even though, internally, her heart had begun to pound.

The arrival of these first proper cramps signified that she was getting closer. Closer to becoming a single mother.

It was her due date, and she'd chosen to work right up to her delivery. She needed the money. The tips she got from working, as well as her wages, if she was going to get by on her own.

The father, Jake, was *not* around. He'd once been a regular customer at the café. Coming in every day on his way to work at the bank, smiling and flirting with her until she'd agreed to a date with him. He had charmed her and let her fall in love with him. Then she'd announced the unexpected pregnancy and he had announced, also unexpectedly, that he was actually married. And had three children. Broken-hearted, she had decided to continue with the pregnancy. Jake had promised to provide financial aid, but nothing else.

As the rest of her shift continued the Braxton Hicks became more regular, and when the café had closed, and she'd helped clean up and mop the floor, her boss told her to get herself off home. She promised she would text him when she got home safely.

She was prepped and ready for anything. Her hospital bag was already in her car, alongside the child seat she would need when she drove home afterwards. The maternity hospital was only a twenty-five-minute drive away. She'd practised. She needed to be prepared for anything, anytime, especially as she was on her own.

And then it began to snow.

Julia smiled as she stepped from the café and turned her face up to the sky, her hands out to catch the softly falling flakes. This was perfect! Christmas Eve… Snowing… It was almost magical. Typically, the snow wasn't settling, as it had rained earlier, but that didn't stop the wonder of it.

As she got into her car, stretching out her seatbelt to fit around her abdomen, she hummed along to the Christmas music blasting from the radio and imagined herself telling her child, in the future, about how it had begun to snow the magical Christmas that he had been born.

She was trying to remain upbeat about the fact that she was going to do this alone, but as she drove through the busy streets, getting stuck in slow-moving traffic, she began to realise that her Braxton Hicks were more than just tightenings. They were beginning to hurt much more…like really bad period pains.

I think I might be in labour.

She tried to remain calm as she sat in traffic that was now at a standstill. Bumper to bumper. Her windows were beginning to fog. Was this truly happening? Now? Today?

Julia called her mum on her hands-free unit and

explained the situation as another pain hit. And then another.

Her mum sounded so excited. 'It's happening?'

Julia smiled at hearing the excitement in her mum's voice. 'Yes, I think so. Pains are coming every few minutes already. Is that normal?'

At her antenatal classes the midwife had said first labours were long. Slow. Usually.

'There's no rulebook for babies, Julia. Is it safe for you to be driving?' asked her mum, clearly worried.

'I'm not driving right now. I'm sat here and I haven't moved in ages! Oh, God, what if I give birth in my car?'

'Is there a shortcut you can take?'

'Maybe...'

The next contraction hit hard whilst she was at a red traffic light. It hit like a vice, squeezing her, crushing her, making her gasp, and was just easing off as the lights went green and she found herself creeping forward at a snail's pace. It was rush hour, so traffic was to be expected, but the intensity of that last contraction had scared her.

She glanced ahead, trying to see past the cars. Was this just volume of traffic, or an accident, or what? This was the main route to the hospital, but what with the snow and all the shoppers it looked as if they were going nowhere, and it was starting to make Julia panic a little. She wanted to be moving. Wanted to be driving so that she could get closer to the safety of the hospital, its midwives and its medications.

She'd planned an epidural. At least, that was what she hoped for, if she needed it.

I could take that left turn up ahead. It would lead me down the country roads and through Weston, so I could get to the hospital that way...

Julia turned on her indicator and when the traffic had moved forward enough for her to take it she took the next exit and began to drive again, feeling good about her choice as the road here was clear. The wipers were dealing with the snow, and though the roads looked dark and slick she was doing okay.

She made it to Weston, drove through the village and out the other side and took the turning that would lead her to the hospital. She was doing great until she heard a strange bang, and then a *thud-thud-thud* with every rotation of her tyres and realised she'd got a flat tyre.

'No!'

Julia pulled over, switching on her hazard lights and getting out of the car to take a look. It was the back tyre, passenger's side, and if she wanted to change it—if there was even the possibility of changing it—she would have to do so from a ditch that was full of ice-cold muddy water and spiky brambles.

She cursed and grabbed her phone, but when she tried to dial for help saw she had no signal and no bars. This had to be a black spot.

She groaned and bent double as another contraction hit.

This one was stronger than any she'd had before and Julia sank to her knees from the sheer force of it, breathing it away as much as she could, the way she'd been taught in antenatal class. It seemed to last for ever, and just when she thought it was over, just when she thought she could breathe normally again, her waters broke and gushed down her legs.

'Oh…'

Don't panic. Don't panic!

But she couldn't help it. She was alone, cold and wet, and in labour. On Christmas Eve, shivering in the snow, with a flat tyre and no way nor ability to fix it and no phone signal.

I need someone to help. Is there a house around here?

She'd seen a house about a mile back, but she couldn't recall if there'd been lights on to show there was anyone there. If she turned back and everyone was out… Lots of people went out on Christmas Eve. To church. To parties. To visit family and friends.

As she got to her feet she thought she could see warm yellow lights up ahead. Something through the trees…

There was no other choice. She couldn't have her baby here on the road. Screw that midwife saying first babies took a long time to arrive. Her son seemed to be in one hell of a rush to be born.

Another contraction hit her, making her collapse against her car before she could get back to her feet and begin to stagger down the road. Julia kept trying to call her mum, or the emergency services, but now her phone seemed to have died, and she was beginning to think the universe was conspiring against her.

The lights were getting brighter, but she could see now that they were from a house set back from the road, up a long and winding driveway.

'You've got to be kidding me!' she gasped, and then another contraction hit, and towards the end of it she felt the urge to push. 'No. No, no, no, no!'

Her freezing breath billowed around her, but Julia got back to her feet and found from somewhere the strength to dig deep and keep on walking.

The house was right there in front of her. Getting closer. It looked like some kind of manor house, or something. It had a Christmas tree outside. Lit up by white fairy lights and topped with a giant silver star that drew her eye. Almost delirious, she laughed and wondered if Mary had felt this way in Bethlehem. Looking for a place to give birth and being guided by a star. Though there'd been no mention in the bible of her terrible contractions, and she'd managed to sit on the back of a donkey...

Ten metres.

Five.

Julia finally reached the door and reached up for

the giant knocker, shaped like a lion's head. She rapped it as hard as she could, groaning against the wood.

'How are you doing now, Doe?'

Anthony Fitzpatrick, Duke of Weston, cradled his wife Yael's hand in his and looked up into her gorgeous big brown eyes.

He had begun to call her Doe because since her chemotherapy, and losing all her hair, her eyes had somehow seemingly become larger and more doe-like. They were beautiful, just as she was.

'I'm a little warmer.' Yale adjusted the oxygen cannula in her nose and pulled the blanket around her.

He knew she would like to get closer to the open fire he'd got going in the living room that had become their bedroom since she'd been wheelchair-bound, but he didn't want to risk it. Not now that she was permanently attached to her oxygen canister.

'Good. Can I get you anything? A hot chocolate? Cocoa?'

She smiled at him and shook her head. 'Just you.'

He smiled back. 'Always.'

Anthony laid his head upon her shoulder and stared into the flames. He tried not to think about how many days they had left together. Two weeks ago the oncologist had told them that the cancer had now spread to her brain, liver and bones. The fluid on her lungs was getting worse, and he'd estimated that she had only weeks to live. Not months. *Weeks.*

This would be their last Christmas together.

Their last days together.

He wanted to make every precious moment count.

The orange flames licked at the fresh logs he'd only recently put onto the fire and his gaze lifted to the two stockings that hung there. They'd once hoped to add to the number of stockings on the mantelpiece, but cancer had put paid to that idea. Endless rounds of chemo, radiation, surgery, immunotherapy and clinical trials had ravaged his wife's body and dashed any hopes of fertility or children.

A rapid knocking at the front door made him lift his head from his wife's shoulders.

'Who's that?' Yael asked.

He laid his head back down again. 'It doesn't matter. Probably just carol singers.'

'Anthony! You should go and answer the door. If they've come all this way out into the country they've made an effort to sing for their duke.' She smiled at him and lifted a weary finger to stroke his jawline. 'The least we can do is give them an audience, and I think I'd like to hear them sing.'

'All right.' He smiled at her, once again amazed at his wife's boundless compassion and love for the festive season, despite all that was going on.

He got to his feet, made sure her blanket was tightly tucked about her, and then wheeled her through to the front hall, parking her just behind him so she'd have a good view of the carol singers, but not so close to the door that she'd feel the cold. The snow had become sleet now, and it was chilly out there.

Odd, though. He couldn't hear anyone singing. Did they wait these days for whoever was in to open the door before they started singing?

Anthony turned the key and swung the front door wide, forcing a jolly smile for whoever was out there. But as the door swung inwards it brought with it a woman, who sagged to her knees groaning, her long dark hair wet like rat's tails.

As she rolled onto her side he realised she was heavily pregnant.

And about to give birth.

A pair of strong arms scooped her up and then she was being carried. And although she longed to just close her eyes and go to sleep, another contraction hit.

'I need to push!'

'Don't push! Not yet!' the man carrying her said.

But it wasn't something she could fight. Her body began to push all on its own and she grunted as she bore down.

The man carried her to a bed and laid her upon it. She thought she heard the tell-tale snap of disposable gloves being put on. Where was she?

Julia opened her eyes briefly and glanced around.

The room was a strange mix of palatial grandeur and hospital ward, and the man beside her, snapping on the gloves, was tall, handsome and darkly bearded.

'I need to examine you. Make sure you're fully dilated. But don't worry—I'm a doctor.'

A doctor? She glanced around for some sort of confirmation, but what she expected to see she wasn't sure. Was she hoping to see a certificate on the wall? Would that be enough to allow her to let this strange man remove her clothes and examine her intimately?

But then a woman wheeled herself into view. A frail woman. Young, but bald. A cannula in her nostrils was feeding her oxygen. Julia's first thought was that she must be a cancer patient. But the thought wasn't there for long. Another contraction hit and she gasped and sucked in air, ready to push once again.

'Okay. No time for that, I guess,' the man said, and she felt his hand rest upon her bump, almost as if he was measuring the strength of the contraction. 'Yael, can you pass me those clean towels over there? And I'll need those scissors.'

Julia heard packets being ripped open, things being placed beside her on a metal instrument trolley, and then the rest of the world disappeared as all she could feel was the pain and constriction of her latest contraction. She gasped and cried out, before sucking in more air so she could hold her breath and push. Push harder than she'd ever pushed in her life.

'That's it…you're doing great. I'm sorry, but I'm going to have to remove your underwear. Do you give me permission?'

She nodded furiously, not caring any more as she felt hands beneath her skirt and she lifted and twisted so that her knickers could be removed. Who cared what this strange man saw? Or did. Or touched. All that mattered was getting this baby out of her body. She felt as if she was on fire. As if she was being torn in two.

'Head's out! One more big push and you're done!'

The head was out! It was nearly over!

The thought gave her one last surge of energy—of strength—and she groaned and sucked in air for one final big push. And then, with a big whoosh of fluids, her son slithered out of her and was lifted onto her belly by the bearded man.

Julia looked down, crying, holding her son's hot, wet body as the strange man whose home she'd barged her way into began to rub her baby down with towels, clearing away blood and mucus and vernix, the natural white grease that coated a new baby's skin.

'Why isn't he crying?'

'He will. Give him a moment.'

She looked up at the man properly this time. She saw worry, concern, in his bright blue eyes, but he was staying calm, seemed certain of what he was doing, and she had no choice but to believe him.

To place her faith in him.

To trust him.

Not only with her life, but with her son's.

And then…

'Waah!'

The baby began to cry and she sobbed happy tears, holding her son to her, unable to believe all that had happened in the last hour or two. The tears combined with the relief that he was here and he was okay and she'd got through it all.

'Let me clamp and cut the cord,' the man said, before wrapping her son in another clean towel and putting him into her arms.

He was beautiful. Red. Plump. A button nose. A gummy mouth. Squinting every time he tried to open his eyes and look out at the world. He sneezed and looked bewildered, and Julia couldn't help but laugh at him before looking up at the man whose home she had invaded. At the bald woman in her wheelchair with her oxygen. They were both looking at her in awe and wonder.

'Thank you for letting me in. For answering the door. My name's Julia… Julia Morris.'

'And who's this little guy?' the man asked.

'I'm going to call him Marcus, after my grandfather. Marcus Arthur Morris.'

The man and the woman smiled. The woman

in the wheelchair looked almost mesmerised by the baby.

'We never got a chance to be properly introduced, did we? My name's Anthony, and this is my wife Yael.'

Julia smiled and said hello, before looking down at her son again. He was so beautiful…

'I'll call for an ambulance. Get you both checked out.'

'There's no phone signal here,' Julia said.

'We have a landline.'

'Oh. Thank you.'

'You're welcome.'

The man removed his gloves and went to the opposite side of the room, where he picked up a phone handset, dialled and requested an ambulance. When he came back, he put on fresh gloves.

'For the placenta,' he explained.

'Oh, right. I forgot that part.'

'You'll hardly notice now you've got that little guy in your arms.'

He was right. She hardly did.

'The ambulance might be a while. It's Christmas Eve…they're busy. Can I get you anything, Julia? Water? Some tea?'

'Tea would be great, thank you. Thank you both for this…for going to so much trouble. I hope I haven't made a mess of your rugs or anything.'

Yael wheeled herself forward. 'Don't worry about that. Is…is he your first?'

Julia nodded, wondering whether she ought to try and breastfeed. 'Yes.'

'You'll always find Christmas special from now on.'

'I guess I will.'

His birthday was Christmas Eve. She'd never thought it would happen this way when the doctor had predicted her due date. 'First babies are always late,' she'd been told. He would more likely be a New Year baby. Or early January.

'He'll get two lots of presents,' said Yael.

She smiled. 'He'll get spoilt. My mother will go overboard, no doubt.'

'And his father? Will he be surprised?'

Julia turned to look at Yael. 'I'm not with him any more. He didn't want to know.'

'I'm sorry. I didn't mean to pry.'

'Don't worry. You didn't know.'

She looked around the room. Noted the opulent paintings. The long, heavy drapes. The expensive vases on the mantelpiece that was decorated with pine, fir cones and fairy lights. Two solitary stockings hung there.

'Do just the two of you live here?'

It was a big house. Huge for just two.

'Yes. We'd hoped to start our own family, but then this happened.' Yael fiddled with her oxygen tubing, looking embarrassed.

'Do you mind if I ask…?'

Yael shook her head kindly. 'Non-small cell lung cancer. It's metastasised.'

'Oh. And can they…do anything about it?'

Yael smiled. 'I'm fighting it. The doctors are throwing everything at it.'

'That's good.'

'Yeah. It is.' She looked down then, almost incredibly sad, and Julia wondered if the woman knew more about her condition than she was letting on.

Was the disease winning? Was it beating her? Was it killing her? She'd hoped to start a family with her husband—what was his name? Anthony? What if they couldn't? What if time was running out for them? What if this was Yael's last Christmas?

'Would you…like to hold him?'

Yael looked up, her eyes full of wonder and surprise. 'You don't mind?'

'Of course not. Here, come closer and I can pass him to you.'

Gently and carefully she passed her son down into Yael's waiting arms. She gasped as she took the baby, and looked at him so tenderly and with so much love he might as well have been her own baby.

'Tea.' Anthony came in bearing a tray, and suddenly stopped moving when he saw his wife cradling the baby.

Julia couldn't possibly describe the look on his face when he saw them. Gratitude? Happiness? Joy? Awe? Maybe it was all of them? And more.

He placed the tray down on the table and then went to kneel by his wife's side. They held Julia's son together, as if he were their own. They looked like *they* were the new parents and she the surrogate. It made Julia's heart swell that she could do this for them.

'I can't thank you both enough for what you have done for me and my son tonight.'

Anthony looked up at her as he cradled Marcus's head. 'You're very welcome.'

'I was lucky to find a doctor, I guess.'

He smiled at her, and she had to admit that he was rather handsome. Yael had struck lucky in the husband department. It was ironic that Yael had something that Julia had hoped for and she had something Yael and Anthony had hoped for. Life was strange that way.

When the ambulance and the paramedics finally arrived and she was being loaded into the ambulance she waved goodbye to Anthony and Yael, thanking them one last time for all that they had done.

They stood in the doorway of their manor house and even though they had each other, Julia couldn't help but feel that they looked incredibly alone. Their arms empty of her son, they looked lost.

She could only hope, as she was driven down the long driveway, that she had brought a little Christmas magic to their home. That they would always remember the Christmas they'd helped a stranger deliver her baby in their living room and that they would have many more Christmases together.

CHAPTER TWO

Present day

'HELLO? I'M LOOKING for the nurse in charge?'

Julia stood by the reception desk of the orthopaedic ward, smiling at the receptionist. The ID on a lanyard around her neck stated that her name was Mandy.

'And you are…?'

'Julia Morris. Newly qualified nurse. I start work here today.'

She beamed, still quite unable to believe she was saying it.

Newly. Qualified. Nurse.

It had felt incredibly strange going to university to study. Most of the rest of her class had been young girls. Teenagers, really. Eighteen years of age. Nineteen… She'd been about to turn thirty, but she'd not been the oldest by any means. There'd been one woman studying who'd just turned forty years old. She and Cesca had become really good friends, actually, which was nice, and Cesca was starting today, too, up on the Gynae Ward.

Julia's life had changed so much in the last few years. It had almost been a whirlwind. But now she was sure of her choices. She'd enjoyed her working placements on the orthopaedic ward where she'd trained, and she hoped she would enjoy it just as much here at London's Saints' Hospital.

'Oh, yes, I was told to expect you!' Mandy passed her a sticky note with a number on it. 'Go down that corridor to the end and you'll see a sign that says *Staff Only*. Type in that number and it'll get you inside, where you can meet everyone for morning handover.'

'Thank you.'

Julia adjusted the backpack on her shoulder and headed down the corridor. It was bright here. Modern. The hospital had just had a major revamp that must have cost millions. She couldn't help but glance into the wards as she passed them by. Most of the beds were filled. Men in one ward. Women in another. She passed a door marked *Linen*, another marked *Utility* and then she was at the *Staff Only* door. There was a keypad on it, and she typed in the number and turned the handle, sucking in a breath for courage, knowing that she was about to meet the people who would become her work family for the next few years.

But as she turned the handle to push it forward the door was pulled back by someone exiting, and she bumped into a tall man by accident, backing away, blushing, full of apology...before she looked up to make eye contact and her heart almost erupted from her ribcage.

The man before her did not seem to have changed much since she had last seen him a decade ago. His hair was a little longer, but otherwise he looked exactly the same as when he and his wife Yael had waved her goodbye from the door of their home. Now he wore a slim-fit navy suit, with a white shirt and pink tie, a waistcoat rather than a blazer, and a stethoscope draped around his neck. His gaze grazed over her in an automatic apology, but then his eyes widened with recognition.

He recognises me. He remembers me.

'Anthony! Hello, again.'

He seemed to take a moment to think, and Julia stood there, smiling, holding out her hand in greeting, as surprised as he to have remade his acquaintance.

'It's *Mr* Fitzpatrick,' he said, his voice gruff, and he avoided shaking her hand and walked straight past her, as if they had never shared something special at all.

Julia gaped after him, shocked and a little embarrassed at having been dismissed so easily.

Maybe he doesn't remember me?

But then a nurse dressed in a dark blue uniform, with white piping on her collar and a kind face, got her attention. 'Is it Nurse Morris? Come on in. Don't mind him—he's always grumpy.'

Julia turned to face the room and felt her cheeks

flush even more when she realised that she seemed to be the last person to arrive and everyone had witnessed the interaction. The room was full of people in uniform. Nurses. Healthcare assistants. Student nurses. People whom she assumed were from the physio department, judging by their white polo shirts and navy tracksuits.

'Er...yes. Thank you.'

'I'm Maeve Booker, sister in charge of the ward. Come and take a seat. Sara? Can you budge over, so Nurse Morris can sit down?'

A young blonde nurse got up and moved, so that Julia could squeeze into the seat next to her.

'Thank you.'

'No problem.'

She was passed a handover sheet and she listened intently as a nurse ran through the patients from the nightshift, with a list of jobs that needed taking care of that day. Cannula insertions, medication requests, bloods... Which patients needed to get out of bed that day and ambulating around the ward, which ones were needing to be prepped for surgery, which ones were due to go home. She outlined overnight developments—who had slept well, who hadn't.

It was a lot of information for Julia to take in, but she was used to this. She'd sat in on many handovers during her placements as a student nurse. She scribbled down notes relating to each patient, so that she had a good idea of what needed to be achieved that day, and could try to understand the new problems and requirements that might crop up, or new patients who might arrive.

Afterwards, as everyone filtered out, Maeve grabbed her attention and waved her over.

'Do I call you Julia? Jools? What do you prefer?'

'Either is fine.'

'Okay. Obviously we need to orientate you, as it's only your first day, so why don't you work with some of the HCAs this morning, helping to get the patients washed and fed? That way you'll get to know who we've got and meet them all. Well, as many as you can get to. And then, later on, you can help with some of the duty list—how does that sound?'

'Perfect.'

'Great.' Maeve stood, pushing her handover sheet into her uniform pocket and looking at her curiously. 'You know Mr Fitzpatrick?'

She blushed again, not sure she wanted to share how exactly she knew him. 'Er…we met once. Years ago now. He probably doesn't remember.'

'Professionally? Or socially?'

'Socially.'

'Oh, okay… He's a great doctor. An orthopaedic surgical consultant. We all call him Mr Ice, because he keeps everyone at a distance. Never socialises. Never hangs around to gossip or chew the fat. He keeps himself to himself, to be fair.'

'So it wasn't just me, then?'

'No!' Maeve laughed. 'Definitely not. There are a lot of young nurses and other staff who wish he would be friendlier, though.'

Julia could understand why. Anthony was a very handsome man.

'Right, let's give you a bit of a tour. Show you where everything is.'

'Sounds good.'

She was raring to go and to put the discord of meeting Anthony—*Mr* Fitzpatrick... *Mr Ice*—to bed. This was a new start for her. The beginning of a brand-new chapter in her life. She wanted to do well, and her little faux pas with Anthony Fitzpatrick was not going to ruin that.

It had been a long nightshift and he'd been ready to go home. To sleep. To eat. To rest. He'd just been dropping off some surgical aftercare orders for an emergency that had come in through the London Saints' A&E department to Maeve before he went home. As he'd reached to pull the door open it had been thrust towards him, and then someone had run into his chest.

A nurse. Shorter than he was. With dark brown hair tied up in a bun.

When she'd looked up to apologise he'd recognised her instantly. No rat's tails of wet hair, no ruddy cheeks from the cold, cold snow, no pregnant belly and no baby about to make its entrance into the world. But of course he'd known who she was! Instantly. Because he'd often thought about that night.

Delivering babies wasn't in his remit at all, but he was a doctor, and he knew what to do, and he'd been so thankful that there hadn't been any complications. No postnatal haemorrhage or problems with the baby. But what he most remembered from that night was the gift she had given his wife. Letting Yael hold her son.

Yael had dreamed of having her own baby. Of carrying it in her womb, how the birth might be, how they'd be a little family afterwards and what great parents they would make. And Julia had allowed her a precious moment, a perfect Christmas gift, that Yael had spoken of many times after their surprise guest had been whisked away in an ambulance.

How she'd missed the feel of that baby in her arms. She'd allowed herself to imagine that the baby was hers. For just a little while. Knowing that it would be her only chance to hold a newborn baby like that. How perfect the little baby boy had been. How good it had felt to hold him. How it had lifted her heart and her mood after the news that they'd got a few days previously that she only had a few weeks left to live...

He'd not known Julia was a nurse. She'd never said. And he'd most definitely not expected to find her going into that staffroom. Did she work here now? Would he have to see her every day at the hospital?

The thought disturbed him.

She disturbed him.

He liked to keep his private and personal life away from work. He didn't need her blabbing about the incident to all and sundry. He'd have to have a word with her about it. Quietly. Somewhere private, where no one else could hear. The hospital grapevine was a vibrant, healthy thing. And she'd called him *Anthony.* In front of his colleagues. As if she knew him. Which she *did.* But he couldn't have her calling him by his first name here. It had felt…strangely intimate. A shock.

And had she always been that beautiful? Ten years ago he'd not really focused on her looks. Her long hair had been down, and loose, but it had been soaking wet, covering her face every time she pushed, her face squeezed tight, the skin flushed and red, wet from the cold, rounded with pregnancy.

Even after the birth, when she'd held her son in her arms, he'd never truly seen her real features.

Now her hair was swept up neatly, away from her face. Her eyes were a deep brown colour, large and wide—

Like Yael's.

The unbidden comparison arrived in his brain almost gleefully.

Doe.

But Julia's face was slimmer, her cheeks a soft,

rosy pink. Her smile wide, her lips soft-looking. It had taken him a moment to recognise her, and when he had—when she'd used his name so easily—he'd felt so broadsided, so shocked, that he'd corrected her, not wanting their intimacy to be shared so publicly.

What am I going to do?

He would have to find a way to deal with working with her each day.

If I just treat her the way I treat everyone else then I can keep her separate and away from my life, like the other people I work with. It will be that simple.

Right?

The next day Julia was with her first patient, a Miss Tiffany Morello, who'd arrived on the ward from A&E that morning after falling. She had a broken tibia and fibula in her left leg that needed surgical plating and required the insertion of a cannula in preparation for surgery.

'What were you doing up a lamppost?' Julia asked as she swabbed the skin with an alcohol wipe. She'd already found the vein easily.

Miss Morello blushed. 'It was silly, I know, but I wanted to get a good view of Patrick Delacourt going into his hotel.'

'Who?'

'Patrick Delacourt. The actor. He's been in all those action movies...recently divorced and *single*!'

Julia smiled. She'd never heard of him. 'And so you climbed a lamppost?'

'I climbed a lamppost. I had no choice. I'd been waiting for ages, but all the paparazzi were there, and they had stepladders to see over each other and they blocked my view. So I thought, *I could shimmy up that lamppost and then I'll see him and maybe he'll see my banner.*'

'You made a banner?'

Tiffany smiled. 'It read *Patrick do you wanna court me?* And then my phone number.'

Julia laughed. 'Brave.'

'Or stupid. I thought I could hold on to the lamppost with one hand and wave my banner with the other when he arrived. But I slipped and fell and heard something snap.'

'Ouch.'

'Yeah…'

'Has he called?'

Tiffany pouted. 'No.'

'Maybe he'll hear about it and make a secret visit to you in hospital?'

Her patient suddenly brightened. 'Do you really think so? I should put something on social media and tag him into it!'

As her patient grabbed for her phone Julia heard the arrival of the doctors on the ward to do their round. She turned to look, as she cleared away after the cannula insertion, and noted Mr Fitzpatrick was leading the charge, surrounded by registrars and juniors.

He looked very commanding. An alpha male if ever there was one. And if she hadn't met him before, and seen his soft, encouraging side, she would probably have been a little afraid of him. But his bedside manner was amazing. She'd been on the receiving end of it, and she knew there was warmth within that Mr Ice personality.

'Who's presenting?' he asked his assorted juniors, without even looking at Julia. It was almost as if she wasn't there.

One of them raised a hand. 'Miss Tiffany Morello, twenty-two years of age, presented in A&E just after eight o'clock this morning after falling from a height of approximately eight feet. X-rays in the department demonstrated displaced fractures of both the tibia and fibula of the left leg.'

Julia watched as he was passed a tablet and he called up the X-ray images to examine them more closely.

Then he looked up at his patient and smiled. 'Miss Morello, I'm Mr Fitzpatrick, and I'm going to be operating on your leg later today. You've been told you need surgery?'

'Yes.'

'My plan is to do an open reduction and internal fixation of the bones. What that means is that we'll do an open surgery to realign and set your bones with screws and plates, to facilitate the healing and stability of the leg to bear weight for walking.'

'Will it be a general anaesthetic?' Tiffany asked nervously.

'Yes. An anaesthetist will come along shortly to talk to you about anaesthesia, but a general is the best solution with this sort of surgery.'

'Is it an easy fix?'

He nodded. 'Generally. Of course we can never know the true extent of an injury until we get inside, but it's usually a run-of-the-mill operation for us. I understand that it's not for you, and that you may have some concerns or worries. I'd be very happy to talk you through them, if you like?'

'I've had a surgery before. My appendix...' Tiffany explained, blushing.

Julia couldn't help but notice how Tiffany was looking at Mr Fitzpatrick.

'Good. You should also know that after this surgery it can take anything from six to eight weeks to heal. You'll be given crutches, and physiotherapy to assist you afterwards. Do you have family or friends who can help you?'

'I live with my mum and dad. Still.'

He smiled. 'Nothing wrong with that. Now, just promise me that you won't slack on the physio afterwards. It's a comprehensive programme that should maximise the effectiveness of the surgery and give you full function, reduce any pain or stiffness you might experience and enable you to go climbing again.'

Tiffany laughed. 'Oh, I won't be climbing any more lampposts, let me tell you!'

'Glad to hear it. Now, if you have any questions then...' he turned and finally looked at Julia '... Nurse...?'

'Morris,' she said, her cheeks flushing.

'Nurse Morris will be able to contact me and I'll try and come and talk to you again. If not, I'll see you after the surgery, all right?'

'Thank you, Doctor.'

He gave his patient a nod, briefly looked at Julia, then moved on to the patient in the next bed.

Julia felt utterly deflated. She had thought that he might find time to come and talk to her, since running into her yesterday, but she'd learned that he'd been on a nightshift and had gone home. She'd then had a sleepless night of her own, wondering what shift he was on today, before she came into work wondering if they would have time to talk. She dearly wanted to ask him how his wife was doing, though if she did that she knew she'd have to talk about Marcus...

But it would be nice just to have a moment with him. Check in with him...see how he was doing and what he'd been up to these last ten years.

Had his life changed as much as hers?

She'd often wondered.

The urge to talk to him now that she knew he was

here was strong. Although only a tiny part of Marcus's life, he had been there when she'd brought him into the world and that meant something. He'd saved her from having to give birth on a freezing wintry night in the middle of the countryside. Open to the weather. He'd brought her into his warm home and delivered Marcus safely.

They had a connection.

They would always have it.

And somehow him being here made her feel close to her son once again. She felt a wave of sadness slam into her, almost taking away her breath, but then it was gone.

But what about that moment before, when he'd turned to her and asked her surname as if he didn't know it? She'd told him all those years ago. He knew her last name. Why pretend he didn't? To show everyone else that he didn't know her all that well after she'd called him Anthony?

It's been ten years. Maybe he thinks I got married?

It was a possibility.

Julia watched as he went around the ward, finishing his round, and when he went over to the reception desk to write notes in a file she swallowed hard, gathered some courage and went to stand beside him, leaning on the counter and deliberately looking at him, waiting for him to notice her.

'Can I help you, Nurse Morris?'

He continued to write. Didn't even look up. Why was he acting this way?

'Yes, you can.'

He closed the file, handing it to the receptionist, and then turned to look at her, one eyebrow raised. 'How?'

Now she was flustered. They might have shared a very intimate moment—a gargantuan moment in her life that she would always remember—but it was over a decade ago now, and it wasn't as if they were friends. They'd never kept in touch. Though she'd always meant to. It wasn't as if they had any obligation to each other, but she couldn't understand why he was talking to her the way that he was.

'I just… We shared something. A long time ago, I'll admit, but we shared an amazing moment together. And you and Yael were so…welcoming and kind and warm. Yet now I'm feeling confused, because you're…'

Should she call him cold? Distant? Unapproachable? Terse?

Anthony glanced at the receptionist, whom she saw was thankfully on a call and not listening to them at all.

'We are at work, and work requires us to be professionals,' he said quietly.

'I know that. Lives are in our hands. But we can be professionals and still be nice to one another.'

'You don't think I'm being "nice"? When was I mean?'

'You haven't been. It's just…your tone,' she said awkwardly.

'My *tone*?'

'You know they all call you Mr Ice?'

'I do. It's respectful.'

'Is it?'

Or maybe it signalled the fact that they thought he was the most unapproachable person they'd ever met?

Annoyed, she began to walk away. Flustered. Frustrated. Angry. Why had she even thought that they could be friends? Clearly the warm, kind and wonderful man she'd met on Christmas Eve all those years ago no longer existed. Was it because of something bad? Had he lost Yael?

She stopped walking as her mind filled with the memory of Yael. Wheelchair-bound. Thin. Frail. Bald. Using oxygen for her non-small cell lung cancer.

Julia turned back to face him. 'I've been wondering… I've been worried. How's Yael?'

His eyes darkened and she saw a muscle clench in his jaw.

'She's dead.'

CHAPTER THREE

THERE HAD BEEN no time to explain more, so he'd taken her quietly to one side and told her he'd meet her in the hospital canteen at lunchtime. Her lunch was at one, so he'd got his consults finished by then and now he sat at a table, nursing a coffee, thinking about how he would tell Julia what had happened.

He'd not shared the exact details with anyone here. They knew, of course, that his wife had died ten years ago, but they didn't know more than that. His private life was exactly that, and he refused to be the subject of pity or sympathy. The only way he could get through each day was to work hard, ignore gossip and keep himself to himself. Build walls. Keep people out. Keep people from getting close. That was what worked, and it was what kept him strong. His patients—the people who needed him—were what kept him going. They were his focus. Not his tragic past. The fact that he was now going to share what happened with someone at work felt very strange indeed.

Why her?

Why was he willing to tell *her* the truth?

Because she'd met his wife? Because she and Yael had talked? Because Julia had known what was going on with her cancer? Or was it because of the baby? The happiness that Julia had given his wife that magical Christmas night. As if she had known it would be Yael's only chance to hold a newborn and she had given her that gift selflessly, even when she had probably been very frightened, exhausted and spent after the events of that evening.

He felt he owed her an explanation.

She deserves the truth.

He watched her as she entered the canteen, her eyes scanning the room, looking for him. Saw the way she smiled softly when she spotted him. She grabbed a coffee for herself, placing it on a tray with a couple of plates of food, paid for them and then made her way over to the table.

She passed him a plate with a ham salad on it and fries. 'I figured you hadn't eaten. One of the nurses told me you've only just come out of clinic.'

He smiled and accepted. 'Thanks.'

But he wasn't hungry. Apprehension had obliterated any hunger he'd felt earlier in the day.

She sat opposite him, adding a little salt to her own fries before she looked up at him and smiled. 'So…'

'So.' He watched her face. She looked confused. Concerned. A little curious. 'I apologise for the way I spoke to you when we met yesterday.'

'Oh. Right. Thank you.'

'You took me by surprise. I keep my private life and my professional life separate, and I've never had a nurse call me Anthony.'

'Well, you might have to get used to it. To me, you're Anthony. Not Mr Fitzpatrick. He sounds like a lawyer. Or a judge.'

'I have been known to be judgemental in my time.'

He was finding it difficult not to be abrupt. This was strange for him. Sharing. And it was surprising to realise that he did want to be open with her.

'I'm sorry about Yael. I didn't know,' she said now.

He thought about his wife's doe eyes, so similar to the eyes of the woman opposite. 'Thank you.'

'I take it the cancer…won?'

Anthony looked down at the table. Even after all these years it never got any easier to say it. 'Yes, it did.'

'When?'

'A few weeks after we met you.'

'Weeks?' She looked horrified. 'I'm so sorry!'

'Not your fault. We knew she didn't have long. Those weeks should have been terrible, but in actual fact they were anything but. Yael couldn't stop talking about you and baby Marcus. About how it had felt to hold your son in her arms and pretend for just a moment that he was actually hers. We spoke about you both a lot.'

He let out a breath and ran his hands through his hair, before reaching for his coffee and taking a fortifying sip. His gaze grazed over everyone else in the cafeteria, making sure that no one could see him lose his usual composure.

'I could see it in her eyes,' she said.

'What?'

'That maybe she didn't have long left. Her need to hold him. It seemed like such an easy thing to do…to help another person who was suffering.'

'You know I almost didn't answer the door?'

Julia almost laughed in disbelief. 'Really?'

'I thought you were carol singers. Yael was exhausted. We'd received bad news from her doctors that the latest clinical trial wasn't working and that her treatment cycle was over. I was in no mood to celebrate Christmas. But she—Yael—she wanted to hear some singing. Her last Christmas. She wanted to hear people sing carols.'

'And you got me instead.'

'Better for her than any carol singers, believe me.'

'I'm glad. She looked so happy with Marcus in her arms. The way she took him from me…so reverently, like he was the most precious thing in the world.'

'He was.'

'Yes…' she answered sadly. 'Please tell me she went painlessly.'

'She did. She was on a lot of morphine at the

end. Slept a lot. And then one afternoon she just stopped breathing.'

'It must have been hard.'

He nodded, thinking back to that day. That moment. Sitting by her bedside having watched her chest for hours, having listened to each agonal breath, and then… Silence. Stillness.

'As a doctor, you're so well-trained that when someone's heart stops beating you want to give CPR…you want to start pumping that person's chest to bring them back. But I knew I couldn't bring her back, even if I wanted to.'

'What day did she die?'

He looked up at her. 'February eighteenth. Four days after Valentine's Day.'

He didn't understand the shock that registered on her face.

Or why her hand trembled as she lifted her mug of coffee to her lips.

'What's wrong?' he asked.

How to tell him? How to tell him about Marcus?

Just say it? The way he had about Yael?

There'd been no messing around—*'She's dead.'*

Was it easier to say it if the person who had died had been an adult? Someone who had experienced life, who'd had cancer, so maybe it was expected and not a surprise? It was surely harder to say when the person who had died was still a baby.

'It's Marcus.'

Anthony frowned.

She pushed her plate away, no longer hungry, and took a sip of fortifying coffee. This news never got any easier to say, no matter how many times she had given it. She remembered that early-morning phone call to her mother, when she was still in hysterics. The awkward call to Jake who, even though he'd wanted nothing to do with his son, would still need to know.

'He's…er…passed, too.'

Anthony looked at her in shock. Stunned.

It had been nearly a decade. The pain should be easier to deal with. But there was no timeline on grief. No rule to say that the pain of it should lessen with time. It could still hit her with the ferocity of an explosion. A punch to the gut. A tearing apart of the heart. And she felt that right now. Because Anthony had been there. Anthony had brought her son safely into the world and she… She had lost him.

She felt guilt wash over her, as if she somehow had to apologise to him, even though she knew that feeling was a ridiculous one.

'He was a colicky baby. Had trouble sleeping at night. I didn't mind. He was a beautiful gift and I loved him, and I knew that at some point it would pass. Colic is temporary. But I had many weeks of disturbed nights, and most days I was like a zombie. But we got through them. And when he started smiling at me, at about seven weeks, I couldn't believe I was so lucky to have such a wonderful baby boy.'

That was the easy part. The happy part of her recollection. She needed Anthony to know that she had loved and adored her baby. That she would have done anything for him.

'I tried all sorts of tricks. Colic drops. Rubbing his tummy. Massages. Rocking him. Warm baths before bed. Nothing much worked.'

Anthony said nothing. Just continued to listen intently to her. It gave her the strength to continue, let her know that this was a safe space in which to share her pain.

'The night of February seventeenth I put him down just before midnight. I normally put him to bed at around nine o'clock, but he'd already woken up a few times and I'd paced the house for ages. He seemed to settle then, and I kissed him on the forehead and lay him down in his crib. I fell into my bed without even getting undressed. I was shattered. I hoped to get an hour or so's worth of sleep before he woke up again. But when I opened my eyes the clock said it was six in the morning, and I can remember looking at it, marvelling for a moment. Happy that he'd slept through for the first time ever. And then… I got worried. I've never got out of bed so fast, and I rushed to his room.'

Her voice had begun to wobble. Tremors of emotion were catching in her throat. Tears burned the backs of her eyes. Her hand trembled as she remembered that morning.

'I ran into his room, terrified that something had happened. But another part of me, the logical part, was telling me that I was being ridiculous, and that I'd open his door and see him softly snoozing...all red-cheeked and his face swollen with sleep. But he didn't look like that at all.'

How long had she lingered in the doorway, looking at him? Seconds? It had felt like minutes, with her brain refusing to acknowledge what she could see.

'He was pale. Still. His lips already blue,' she whispered. 'I didn't know what to do! Clearly he wasn't breathing... I remember lifting him up and holding him in my arms, begging him to wake up!'

The tears flowed freely now as the memory of discovering Marcus in his crib came right back to her and placed her in that moment.

'They'd taught us a little infant CPR during our antenatal classes, so I placed him on the floor and tried to remember the right way to do it. Some voice was screaming at me to phone for help first, but I knew that if I did that I would have to leave him to get my phone. So I picked him up again and raced to my bedroom and dialled for an ambulance.' She paused to catch her breath. 'It didn't take them long to arrive, but those moments alone in my bedroom felt like centuries. Nothing I was doing seemed to be helping, and I thought I was hurting him. It killed me with every compression I made on his chest, hoping to make him breathe again. To hear him cry again. I would have given anything to hear him cry again.'

Her tears dropped to the table. Even went in her cooling coffee.

Anthony was pale and still as he listened. Eyes downcast.

'They said it was SIDS. Sudden Infant Death Syndrome. He died on the morning of February the eighteenth.'

'The same day as Yael,' he whispered, so softly she almost couldn't hear his voice.

'The same day as Yael,' she confirmed, as stunned as he by the tragic coincidence.

Yael and Marcus, who had met one amazing, snowy Christmas Eve. Marcus had given Yael one moment of happiness that she'd carried with her to the end of her days. And when she'd passed Marcus had gone too. Almost as if they were joined somehow.

'Maybe she's up there holding him?' Julia suggested, trying to smile through her tears. Trying to find something good in the terrible. 'Maybe she's looking after him for me until I get there, too?'

'I hope so.'

Anthony suddenly seemed to realise that at some point during the telling of her tragic tale he'd reached out and taken her hand. That he'd been leaning in, listening intently, staring at her for a long time. Suddenly he sat back and let go, as if he was aware again of his surroundings. That he was at work and that someone might have seen them together.

She felt his walls go back up, saw the professional mask appear on his face as if by magic. She looked around, too. No one seemed to have noticed them, partially hidden as they were by some fake Yucca trees.

'I met some wonderful nurses who took care of me at the hospital when I arrived. The paramedics must have known Marcus was gone, but they kept working on him until we got to A&E, where the doctors told me there was nothing they could do. Those nurses...they inspired me to become one. Not straight away. I had to process my grief. But eventually, when the time was right, I applied to university and completed my three years training. And here I am.'

'You created something good out of tragedy. You chose to help people.'

She nodded. 'If I can help one person feel better, the way those nurses helped me during my darkest times, then it will help me feel close to Marcus again. Somehow... It makes sense to me,' she said, shrugging a little with embarrassment.

'It makes total sense. You find the light in the dark.'

'That's absolutely it.' She smiled at him. It was a thank-you for his kindness whilst she told him about her son. 'It's strange to still feel like you're a mother when you have no one to care for. This job helps. My placements during training showed me that. Do you…?' She paused, wondering if her question would sound stupid. 'Do you still feel like a husband? Sometimes? Do you…forget?'

Anthony gave a small laugh. 'Sometimes. My mother, on the other hand, is forever reminding me that I am not a husband, and that I have a duty to my seat not only to find myself another spouse, but also to provide an heir.'

Okay, something didn't make sense…

Julia frowned. 'Your seat? An heir? What do you mean?'

Anthony looked at her. 'I'm not just Anthony Fitzpatrick, orthopaedic surgeon. I am also the Duke of Weston.'

'What?'

'It's true.'

'You're a duke?'

She wanted to laugh now. A duke? A real-life duke?

'I am. My mother feels that I have mourned my wife long enough and she is forever trying to set me up with various suitably titled ladies.'

'Wow…'

'I don't want to upset her, but she seriously needs to butt out.'

'So tell her.'

'You've never met my mother. The word *no* is not in her vocabulary.'

'Sounds like my mother…'

'Really?'

'She thinks that the thing to gladden my heart again is for me to get involved with another man. Her response, when she heard I'd got a permanent job in this hospital, was not *Congratulations* but *"Think of all those eligible doctors you'll meet!"'*

Julia laughed wholeheartedly, seeing the mirth in his eyes, too, until her consciousness happily reminded her that in actual fact she was sitting across from a most eligible doctor indeed.

A handsome one.

A widowed one.

A *duke*.

Her laughter died quite quickly and she looked away, hoping he didn't think that she was going to come after him romantically.

'How similar our lives have become,' she said, her voice quiet.

Anthony looked back at her. A strange look in his gaze. 'Indeed.'

CHAPTER FOUR

IT HAD BEEN a most enlightening conversation with Julia. But sad and unfortunate, too. Discovering that Marcus had died had made him incredibly sad, because he'd believed for all this time that the perfect little baby boy who had brought his wife such joy was still out there. Living his life. Being a boisterous ten-year-old. At school. Playing football with his friends. Getting excited about the latest computer game. Streaming. Having fun and laughing and being absolutely, vitally, *alive*.

But he wasn't. He had died the same day as Yael. The two of them somehow bonded together, almost as if they'd been unable to survive without the other. Connected by some strange cosmic cord that had pulled them both into the darkness.

Life was good at throwing curveballs. But he'd put up enough walls to assume that he could avoid any further ones. Just continue to live his life as a doctor. Operate. Help people. Stay professional. Not get attached to anyone or anything.

Mr Ice.

Of course he knew they called him that, and it was fine by him. The name created another wall, because people knew what to expect and not to try to push past it. The only people he remained attached to were his mother and his sister, but his mother was as strong as an ox, and would be around for ages yet, and his sister was newly married and healthy.

His mother was a woman who lived a full life and kept herself busy. Right now she was organising a charity ball at the family seat, to raise money for cancer research, and in six weeks' time she would be flying out to Australia, to visit her sister. Amelia had emigrated years ago, and started a new life in Adelaide. No doubt, though, in those six weeks his mother would still find the time to badger him into finding someone.

'I don't like seeing you alone, Anthony,' she would say.

'I'm not alone. You're here.'

He had moved out of the manor house where he'd been living with Yael after her death. It had held too many painful memories, so he'd moved back into the main house, where the Duke of Weston usually resided.

'You know what I mean...' A pause, then, *'I've invited the delightful Lady Annabella Forsythe for dinner this evening.'*

'Delightful' in his mother's language, meant *available*. Single. Looking to settle down and marry.

Bless her. His mother was a wonderful woman, but she despaired at his staying unmarried and, even though she respected the great love he had for his wife, she most definitely felt he ought to be settling down again. Putting his grief into the past, where it firmly belonged, and looking for something—*someone*—new. Her efforts had ramped up lately, and she'd told him in no uncertain terms that she expected him to bring someone to her ball and he was not to attend alone. That she couldn't bear the idea of leaving him alone when she boarded that plane to Australia.

He'd briefly considered defying her, just to see the look on her face, but did he really want her flying off to Australia angry? What if that was the last time he saw her? And their last words, their last feelings towards one another, were ones of anger?

No. He would have to find someone. But who? Who to trust to understand that it was simply an agreement and not the start of something? Someone who wanted the same thing as he did. To just get through the evening on the understanding that when they said goodbye at the end of the night the peck on the cheek would be a polite thank-you and not a prelude to something more promising.

These thoughts were running through his head as he approached his next patient. He'd performed a hip replacement that morning on Mr Johnathan Carver and he was now doing his post-op. As he approached the patient, he noticed that Julia was beside his bed, checking the man's blood pressure.

'Mr Carver, how are you doing?'

'Not bad, Doc. Bit of a sore throat, but apart from that I feel good.'

'Some people feel that. It's from the tube they use when you're under, and it should pass reasonably quickly. I thought you'd like to know that your surgery went very well. I didn't have any problems at all and you were a model patient.'

'That's good.'

'How's his blood pressure, Nurse Morris?'

She turned and smiled at him as she folded up the blood pressure cuff. 'One thirty over seventy-five.'

'Perfect. You're not feeling any discomfort from the hip?'

'Not yet.'

He smiled. 'We will continue to give you pain relief whilst you're here, and also painkillers to take home. Let me just check your drain.'

He lifted up the blanket to assess the drain. It was working well and had already drained off a little fluid. All looked good.

'Excellent. The nurses and the physios will be around to help you get walking as soon as possible and teach you how to use a crutch or a walking frame to get about. If everything goes well, we'll get you home as soon as we can.'

'Sounds good to me. When will that be, do you think? I'll need to tell my wife.'

'We'll definitely keep you here for the next day, and then we'll assess you again. Most of my patients go home two or three days post op. The physios will talk to you about how you can manage your daily activities and give you home exercises to keep the joint and your limbs supple. We don't want you to stiffen up or develop any other problems.'

Johnathan nodded.

'You know to expect some pain or swelling in your legs and feet?'

'This lovely nurse was just talking to me about that.'

Julia smiled at him. She had a lovely smile. Her brown eyes large and gleaming. He blinked, unable to speak for a moment, as he quizzed himself on why he should notice her smile. Or her eyes.

He cleared his throat. 'It should get better with time. Don't be alarmed by it, unless you think it's excessive. In which case contact my secretary and I'll get you seen. Otherwise you'll need to make an appointment with your GP surgery to get your clips removed in about ten days as long as the wound is healing well. Questions?'

'Will I need any further follow-ups after the clips have come out?'

'Yes, we'll send you a letter two or three months afterwards. But if you follow your instructions, do your exercises and keep moving, I don't see any reason why you should have any further problems.

No driving for six weeks. And no sex for six weeks either.'

Johnathan blushed and gave a mock salute. 'Yes, Doc. Thank you.'

'Look after yourself. Nurse? Let's keep him on observations for the next twenty-four hours, please. Any problems, have me paged.'

'Of course.'

He headed over to the computer terminal to update his post-op details onto Mr Carver's file, but as he stood there, typing, he couldn't help but feel the pull of Julia's orbit as she moved about the ward. Talking to patients. Caring for them. He saw her lay a hand on a patient's arm. She tucked another one in. She gave another a tissue and laughed at something they said. She was brand-new at this, but was showing no nerves, finding ways to engage with people from all walks of life. Knowing when to laugh, when to just be quiet and listen. When to support. She got along with everyone.

Pity I can't ask her to come to the charity ball...

But then a thought assailed him. *Why* couldn't he? She'd be perfect. She wanted her family off her back, too.

The thought wouldn't go away. He tried to imagine himself walking into the ballroom with her on his arm and seeing the look of surprise on his mother's face.

'Nurse Morris?' he said.

She looked up at him, her face relaxing into a smile as she came over to him. 'Yes?'

'I've got a strange request to ask of you.'

'Oh?'

He didn't want to air it here on the ward. 'Can you meet me at the end of the day? It won't take up much of your time.'

She seemed to think about it, then nodded. 'Sure.'

They walked to a coffee shop just down the street from the hospital and settled at a table in the back. Anthony got them both cappuccinos and a chocolate chip cookie each.

He sat across from her, looking a strange mix of intrigued and aloof.

She had no idea what he wanted to ask her. A request, he'd said. A strange request. She'd mulled over it all afternoon and her brain had taken her to some weird places, but now here they were, and she had no idea if she could help him, but she was willing to listen. She'd like to think that she could help.

'Well, I'm here and I'm all ears,' she said.

Anthony let out a sigh, as if he couldn't quite believe he was going to ask what he was going to ask her.

His apparent nerves were making her nervous. What could it be? He looked...uncomfortable. Was he not used to asking for help?

'I was thinking about what you were saying earlier. About what we were *both* saying about the pressures we have from other people to start dating again.'

'Okay...' What was he going to suggest?

'In my situation, I have pressure from my mother. She keeps inviting prospective brides to the house all the time, in the hope that one will take my fancy. The young Lady Annabella Forsythe is particularly forward and has her sights set on me the way a dog wants a bone. Not that I'm saying she's a dog, but...'

He cleared his throat. Pulled at his collar. Clearly uncomfortable. Awkward.

'I've this big charity ball coming up in a couple of days and then my mother's leaving in six weeks to fly to Australia. She keeps telling me she'd like to know that she's leaving me with Annabella... and honestly...? I'm not looking for love right now. I'm not sure I'll ever be looking for love again. I couldn't help but remember what you said about how your mother is pushing you to date, too.'

Julia nodded. She was. Incessantly. She'd called Julia at home just last night, wanting to know if any of the doctors or other specialists had captured her eye yet.

'And I'm guessing you feel the same way? That you don't want to get pushed into anything before you're ready?'

'That's right.' Julia wasn't sure she would ever trust again. She had a history of getting involved with unavailable men. Her father had let her down spectacularly. And Jake, Marcus's father. She'd tried online dating a couple of years ago and though the men she'd met had looked great, their behaviour had not been. Engaged… Looking for a bit on the side… It had been awful. Plus, she'd worked so hard to secure this career for herself. This new start. This new beginning. Her independence meant so much to her, and getting involved with anyone right now would be an utter distraction and stress that she didn't need.

'So what if I suggested a way to solve *both* our problems?' he said.

'How do you mean?'

'We pretend to be dating. You accompany me to the charity ball as my fake girlfriend who I met at work. We socialise together. Are seen together as the perfect couple. Happy… I get Annabella off my back. My mother goes to Australia happy. Your mother is happy, too… And you and I? We know the truth, have a bit of fun for a few weeks without any threat of commitment, and then we part ways, as friends and colleagues.'

He seemed excited by his idea. Julia was intrigued. It sounded like it could work.

'I see… But there would have to be rules, though, right?'

'Absolutely!'

'Like it would never actually *be* a relationship, so no physical stuff?'

She blushed at the thought of kissing him. Touching him. Being affectionate. He was such a handsome man, but in her own head she thought of him as still married. Still in love with Yael. Even though she knew that his wife was gone. They were both single. There was no reason, actually, why she shouldn't think of him as available. But…no. She was in no state of mind to look for a relationship either.

'No. Apart from perhaps the odd kiss to make it believable. Hand-holding. Dancing at the ball, obviously. Maybe we could even have cutesy nicknames for one another?'

'Like Mr Ice?'

Julia smiled but inside she was reeling. The *odd kiss*? She couldn't help but look at his mouth. At his lips. She'd never really noticed before, but they were perfect. His bottom lip looked ideal for biting. Or sucking. She laughed nervously as wicked thoughts rushed through her head, surprising her, because she'd not thought that way in such a long time.

'Well, not that,' he said. 'Not if we're trying to pretend we're into one another.'

Right. Sensible.

'Okay And how would we end it? What would we tell people?'

He shrugged. 'I don't know. That our love for one another burned too bright and too briefly?'

'Erm… That sounds a little cheesy. Too poetic for something that's only going to last for a few weeks.'

'That we just decided to part as friends, then? We realised that we didn't have enough in common?'

She nodded. 'That could work. Sounds more reasonable. We met at work and though we share the same passion to help our patients, it wasn't enough to hold us together?'

'Yes! And if we tell everyone at work that we're dating, too, then it gets everyone off my back there, as well. Though of course we'd maintain the necessary professional boundaries at work.'

Hmm… People knowing about them at work? She didn't like the sound of that.

'I don't think we should do that at work. It wouldn't be good for me or my career. Do you have problems with approaches at the hospital?'

'When you're an eligible doctor? A duke? People assume I'm rich, and that can attract the wrong type of people—so, yes. I certainly get my fair share of offers.'

'*Aren't* you rich, though?'

He shrugged. 'Oh, definitely.'

She laughed at him. At the easy way he said it. As if money wasn't important. Only rich people thought that, she figured, thinking about how she worried about the cost of running her own car, and the fact that she'd been saving up for months just to be able to buy herself some new furniture. He really was from another planet.

'I don't know… It seems a lot. I don't like lying to people.'

'Neither do I. But it would really help me out, and I'd like to help you, too.'

'Can I think about it?'

'Of course! But just so you know…the charity ball is this weekend.'

'In three days' time?'

He nodded. 'And if you agreed you'd need a ball-gown.'

A ballgown. That sounded expensive.

He must have seen the look of doubt on her face. 'I can refund any expenses.'

Julia thought hard. It was a strange proposal, after all! But…maybe it would be fun? Just to accept his offer and go with the flow? Experience Anthony's life a little bit more? He was a good guy, and he'd helped her all those years ago, letting her in to his house and safely delivering her son. She *owed* him. Even after all this time. And a ball sounded grand and fun. It would be nice to step out of her own life for a bit. Celebrate her new start. To get her mother off her back by dating a duke. And if he was willing to pay for it, then why not? And then, when it was over, it would buy her more time to *not* date. To say she was getting over Anthony, or something.

Who would it hurt?

'Okay,' she said, smiling. 'I'm in!'

CHAPTER FIVE

'WHERE ARE WE GOING?' she asked, as he led her to a boutique dress shop in the heart of London. 'Aren't all the shops closing?'

It had taken them some time to negotiate their way through the capital's traffic. It was a busy Thursday evening and everyone was trying to get home.

'I called ahead and Celine is staying open just for us.'

Julia raised an eyebrow in surprise. 'Celine?'

'She is the most talented dressmaker I have ever seen. She's made outfits for royalty.'

'You know I could have just bought a dress from somewhere?'

'I'm sure. But if we're to pull off this illusion for my mother, I really need her to see that you're someone special. A reason that you, just a nurse, caught my eye when I could have had Annabella. Descended from royalty. A millionairess in her own right. Breeder of some of the finest racehorses in all of England.'

'Just a nurse? Right...'

'I didn't mean that in any derogatory sense. Nurses are what keep hospitals running. Without you, we doctors would be nothing.'

'How is your mother going to believe I could afford such a dress on a nurse's salary?'

'I'll tell her we went dress shopping together—which is true. I'll tell her that you tried on many dresses—which will also be true. And that the dress you fell in love with looked so wonderful on you that I, as the perfect gentleman, offered to pay for it for you, despite your protests, because I thought you looked so beautiful in it. Which will also be true.' He smiled. 'All good lies work when they are bathed in elements of the truth.'

Anthony felt certain that their ruse would work on everyone. He would present Julia as a Cinderella. It would be a *fait accompli*. Everyone there would marvel. With the exception of Annabella, maybe. But they would all smile and nod, even if they wanted to grimace, because they would want to be seen as being happy for him after his tragic past.

He knew that those in his social circle talked about him as some tragic widower. *Poor Anthony Fitzpatrick. Heartbroken over the loss of Yael.* Another woman they'd never expected him to marry...

When you were a duke, there was an expectation that you would marry within your social circle. To another titled woman, perhaps? A lady. A viscountess. Yael had been someone he'd met on his travels. In Brazil, of all places. She'd been there on a gap year, working in a kitchen. She'd cooked his meal and when he'd asked to see the chef, to give her his compliments and appreciation, he'd been bowled over by her in an instant.

Coming home with a girlfriend on his arm—a girlfriend who was just a 'normal' person—had surprised everyone, but everyone had fallen in love with her the way he had. She'd just been that kind of lovely person who made everyone smile.

So Julia wouldn't be a surprise. He'd done this before. There was a precedent.

Celine's shop was situated in Mayfair. It had a simple, elegant exterior—dark blue, with her name in hand-scripted gold—and she welcomed him like an old friend.

'Anthony! Such an honour!'

He greeted her with a kiss on both cheeks, then turned to introduce her to Julia.

Celine looked Julia up and down. 'Exquisite! What a figure! Pleasure to meet you, my darling.'

Julia blushed. 'Er…thanks.'

'You said she was beautiful and you weren't wrong, Anthony. Can I offer you both refreshments? I have coffee…wine? Something a little more…celebratory?'

'Julia?' Anthony turned to her and could see that she was looking a little bewildered.

'Erm…would tea be okay?' she asked timidly.

'Of course!' Celine said. 'Black tea? Green? Peppermint? I've actually just this morning got in some salted caramel tea, which is delicious. You should try it!'

'Er…sure.'

He smiled, kind of enjoying her bewilderment.

As Celine disappeared to prepare their drinks he walked over to a dark green dress with a full skirt. He touched the silky fabric. 'See anything you like?' he asked.

Julia looked around her, her gaze sweeping over the shop, a smile settling onto her features. 'I see plenty, but…'

'But what?'

'I don't know what would be right.'

'Celine can help.'

'What about you? You sound like you've been to your fair share of balls. Which do you like?'

'They're all amazing. What I like isn't important. What is important is finding you a dress that makes you feel like a duchess.'

She turned to him. 'You really think we can pull this off?'

Anthony smiled. 'I do.'

Celine came back with a tray and placed it on a side table, pouring out two cups of tea and asking if they wanted sugar or milk. Once the drinks were sorted, Celine gave Julia another look over, turning her this way and that.

'Let me guess…you're a size twelve, right?'

'I usually buy fourteens…'

'But you hide within your clothes! Trust me, you're a twelve.'

Anthony sat down whilst Celine fussed and flitted about Julia and the shop, presenting dresses, holding them up to her to see if they were her colour, putting some to one side for trying on.

'And don't forget we can adjust any garment, add or take away embellishments, in time for Saturday evening.'

'You have so many beautiful dresses, Celine,' Julia said.

'Thank you. But what makes them *truly* beautiful is the woman wearing them!'

Julia walked over to a midnight-blue gown adorned with crystals. 'This is nice.'

'It is—but I think we could find a better colour for you, to make an impact when you enter the ballroom. You have gorgeous chestnut hair. Eyes like chocolate. I wonder if… Yes! What about this one?'

Celine held up a dress in a soft pink. Ballerina pink. With an asymmetrical neckline.

'I'm not sure I could carry that off…'

'Try it and see,' said Anthony.

He wanted to see her in it. And the realisation that he really wanted to see her in it intrigued him. Yes, he wanted that moment of walking into the ballroom with her, and for everyone to gasp in wonder at the mystery woman on his arm, but he also thought that she would look stunning in it, and he wanted that first view all to himself.

It was a thought process that both stunned and terrified him. He'd never thought he could feel this way again.

'Should I?' she asked.

He nodded and sat back in his chair as Julia and Celine headed to the changing room. As he waited, he pondered their plan. Wondered what Yael would have thought of it all and knew that she would have laughed and laughed and told him it was wonderful. A part of him felt that Yael would love that he was doing this with Julia. Because they'd often spoken of her in the weeks after she'd arrived at their house. Wondered about her. How her life was going. Whether they should have exchanged details and kept in touch...

'Ready?' Celine poked her head out from behind the changing room door.

'Absolutely.' His heart was actually thudding. He was excited.

And then he was gasping, getting to his feet as Julia stepped out from behind the door. Celine had done something to Julia's hair—taken it up in some kind of loose twist, exposing Julia's neck and allowing tendrils of curls to fall softly onto her shoulders. The dress itself had looked amazing on the hanger...but on Julia...

His mouth dropped open and he just *stared*. 'You look...'

'Is it too much?'

'No! You look out of this world!'

He barely noticed her blushes as she stood in front of the mirror to see for herself, checking it from all angles, watching as the soft tulle skirt, grazed the floor. Seeing the way the crystals on the bodice caught the light.

'The right necklace and earrings and no one will be able to take their eyes from her all night,' Celine said.

He couldn't take his eyes from her now. Something long dormant stirred within him and his mouth went dry. But then he forced himself to stop gaping as he remembered that this was pretend, and he wasn't looking for any complications right now. This was all about putting Annabella and his mother off the scent.

'Celine gave me these shoes too.' Julia lifted her skirt slightly to reveal a soft pink heel beneath, which arched her foot and shaped her calf muscle.

'This is the one,' he said.

Anthony dropped her back at her flat afterwards. She wondered what he thought of her rented apartment. It was not anywhere near as glorious as his home had been, and she could only assume the ducal seat, where the ball was going to be held, would be even more grand.

But she felt a lot more comfortable here as he

helped her carry in the bags and boxes that contained her outfit for the ball.

'I will come and pick you up Saturday evening. Seven-thirty?' he asked at the door.

'Sounds great.'

'I guess I should have asked this before, but… you can dance, right?'

'I can body pop. Want to see my robot?' She smiled at him.

He laughed. 'You do the robot on the dance floor and everyone will most definitely notice you.'

Julia laughed. 'I can dance. I actually attended dance school for a few years as a kid. We did modern, tap, ballet… Waltz. Latin. I'm sure it's like riding a bike.'

'I don't think I've ever ridden a bike.'

She looked at him. 'You're kidding?'

'I rode ponies.'

Julia bit her lip, trying not to laugh at the disparity in their upbringing. 'Of course you did. So maybe I'll have to teach you one day. As part of our courtship.'

He smiled. 'It's a date.'

'It sure is.'

He didn't kiss her goodbye before she closed the door.

He didn't need to. There's no one here we need to pretend for.

But she still felt weirdly disappointed that he'd not even pecked her on the cheek. Why was that?

Irritation because she was doing him a huge favour? This subterfuge was a very big deal. She didn't normally go out of her way to lie to people. She didn't like lying at all! But where was this disappointment at no kiss coming from? Was part of her dreaming that this could be real?

The confusion and puzzlement she felt was disconcerting. To distract herself, Julia picked up the phone and dialled.

Her mother answered almost straight away. 'Hi, honey, how did your day go?'

'Yeah, not bad. I got to see a really cool amputation today.'

There was a pause. 'You and I have different definitions for the word *"cool"*.'

Julia laughed. 'I guess... How are you and what's-his-name?' Her mother had recently started seeing a guy she'd met at her book club.

'His name's Ray and he's fine. He's taking me out dancing this Saturday night. Some eighties theme night. So I get to dress up in crazy clothes and backcomb my hair. Or crimp it.'

'Oh. That's a coincidence.'

'What is?'

'Well... I'm going out dancing on Saturday night, too. With a guy.'

Her mother gasped in delight. 'Oh, my God! Tell me everything! What's his name? Is he a doctor? Is he handsome?'

'He's called Anthony. Yes, he's a doctor. An orthopaedic surgeon. But he's an ugly troll.'

'Of course he is. I bet he's absolutely gorgeous. A surgeon, huh? Is he rich?'

'Mum! That kind of thing doesn't matter.'

'Oh, doesn't it? Wait…wasn't that guy who delivered Marcus a doctor called Anthony?'

Julia gripped the phone tighter. 'Yes.'

'It's not the same one, though?'

'Actually…it is. He works on my ward.'

Her mother gasped again. 'But you said he had a wife with… Oh. I see.' Georgia Morris sighed. 'So where is he taking you?'

'There's a charity ball. To raise money for cancer research. He's taking me to that.'

'A ball? Sounds expensive. Do you have a dress?'

'I do. When I put it on I'll send you a selfie of me wearing it.'

'Do. What colour is it?'

'Pink. But not bubblegum-pink…more of a soft blush colour.'

'Sounds lovely. When did he ask you out?'

'I don't know… We've kind of been talking all week, really. Catching up with each other over what's happened in our lives over the years.'

'He knows about Marcus?'

'Yes.'

'How did he take it?'

'How does anyone take hearing that kind of news?'

'And he just asked you out?'

'Yes. Why? What's wrong? You've been going on at me for ages to start dating, and now that I am you don't sound happy.'

'I am, honey. Honestly. It's just a surprise, that's all. The connection.'

'He's nice, Mum. Really nice. And he's handsome and employed and decent. That's all you need to know.'

'And you like him?'

'Of course!'

She meant it, too. She did like him. How could she not like him? It was Anthony. He had delivered her baby. He had found room at his inn and let her in on Christmas Eve, when he'd had his own concerns and worries going on. And he had taken care of her. Her and Marcus. He might never have ridden a bike, only ponies, but she liked him. A lot. He was easy to talk to and he'd done his best to make her feel comfortable when they were at Celine's as they'd sipped salted caramel tea—which had been a revelation. And then the subtle way he'd passed Celine his card to pay for the dress, as if it were *nothing*. And she'd seen the price tag!

'Okay. Well…best of luck with it, then. And I might send you a selfie of me in my eighties gear.'

'I bet you still have it in your wardrobe. I bet you've not even had to buy anything for it.' She smiled, trying to bring a note of levity into her voice, to lighten the mood again.

'I may have kept a shoulder pad or two…'

* * *

For the first time since it had been announced Anthony was looking forward to his mother's charity ball. He would have gone anyway. After all, it was for a great cause, and they'd sold all the tickets. He would have gone in Yael's memory, but he wouldn't have enjoyed it. Simply because of the pressure from his mother and Annabella's constant presence at his side as she tried to be delightful. His mother had sent a lot of lovely young women his way, he had to admit, but no one with whom he had truly felt a connection. No one he wanted to get to know more or become intimate with. So he'd remained a widower and thrown himself into his work at the hospital, even become head of the department—because of his skill and dedication, rather than because of his title.

He had a good surgical list today. A fine way to end his work week before the ball tomorrow, and another day to spend in the company of Julia.

He felt strangely relaxed when he was with her. His guard was down. Had been ever since they'd reconnected, really. There was something about the way her arrival in his life had shaped it and how he felt he knew her, even though that couldn't really be true. But he felt he had a new pep in his step as he entered Theatre to work on a scoliosis case.

Scoliosis was a condition in which the spine would twist or curve abnormally. Most cases were relatively minor, and people could live with it without surgery, but in some cases—like the one he had on his table this morning—it was more severe and the curvature was so bad it affected the lung capacity of the patient.

He was busy inserting a steel rod when the door to Theatre opened.

'Mr Fitzpatrick?'

He felt himself straighten at the sound of Julia's voice. Looked up. 'Yes?'

'One of your patients has come into A&E.'

'Which patient?'

'A Mrs Giger? You performed knee replacement surgery on her two weeks ago.'

'Is there a problem with it?'

'She's been in a car accident and the knee in question has been crushed. They're requesting you go down there to consult.'

'Thank you, Nurse Morris.' He refused to call her Julia in front of their colleagues. 'If you could let them know I'm in surgery, but I'll be down as soon as I can. Is Dr Manning, free?'

Dr Manning was one of his surgical registrars.

'He's on the ward.'

'Could you ask him to come in to assist?'

'Of course.'

She disappeared again and he refocused on the patient in front of him. Mrs Giger would have to wait for his attention, unfortunately. He owed it to the patient on his table to give him his full experience and attention.

He'd already got the hooks attached to the vertebrae, and now he could insert the rod to extend the hooks and therefore straighten the spine and create more stability, resulting in more room for the lungs to work effectively. Now he needed to perform the bone grafts to fuse the vertebrae and maintain the spine's new position. Once he was done, his patient would need to wear a brace for a few months to ensure the best healing.

'You needed me?' Dr Manning arrived in Theatre.

'Yes, I need you to check the autograft, please.'

In an autograft a surgeon used bone from the patient's own body, rather than cadaver bone. In this case the best place to harvest it was from the iliac crest on the rim of the pelvic bone.

He and Dr Manning worked well together, and when the complicated parts of the surgery were over Anthony stepped back from the table. 'Can you finish up for me here? I'm needed down in A&E.'

'Of course.'

He left Theatre, scrubbed out, and headed down to check on Mrs Giger. In Majors, he perused the scan results they had on the patient and saw that all the good work he'd done to replace her knee had been destroyed. Her patella was in pieces and she had comminuted fractures of both the lower leg bones.

'Is it salvageable?' asked the department head.

He sighed. 'Possibly. But it's going to take an

awful lot of work—and even if we can help her she could still lose this leg if she develops complications.'

'She's diabetic,' he reminded Anthony.

'Which certainly adds complications...'

Diabetics often had problems with healing wounds. It was something he had discussed with Mrs Giger when he'd replaced her knee.

'I'll go and talk to her. Are her family here?'

'In the waiting room.'

'Put them in the family room. I'll speak to them after I've seen Mrs Giger.'

Anthony grabbed the phone on the desk and dialled up to his own ward.

'Orthopaedics. Nurse Morris speaking.'

He smiled. 'It's Anthony.'

'Hey.'

'Can you contact the admissions nurse and inform her that those patients arriving for my surgical list this afternoon will have to either see Dr Manning or be postponed? I've got an emergency that's going to take up the rest of my day.'

'Of course. Can I help in any way?'

'No, thanks. Oh, actually... I haven't eaten anything, and if I'm going to be in Theatre for a long time I ought to grab something. Could you pop into the hospital shop and grab me a meal deal?'

'Sure. What do you feel like nibbling on?'

He raised an amused eyebrow, surprised by the question, and laughed. 'Er...'

'Oh, wow. Sorry, I didn't mean it that way. I meant—'

She went into some explanation about how she'd just been talking to another nurse about their favourite nibbles, and the word was at the forefront of her mind. But all he could think of was nibbling her neck, which caused a rush of blood to head south so he had to clear his throat and his mind!

'It's fine. Anything will do. I'm not fussy.'

'I hope you didn't think that I meant…something else?'

He smiled. 'Of course not. It was totally innocent.'

'Yes. Good. Thanks.'

He just needed to tell himself that now…

It was the day of the ball and Julia felt nervous. Incredibly so. She sat on her bed, staring at the dress that was hanging on her wardrobe door in a protective cover, and all she could think about was whether they would be able to persuade Anthony's mother and everyone else he knew that he was actually dating *her*.

She'd thought that just mentioning Anthony would blow her mother away, and that she'd be so happy for her she'd get off her back. But instead, ever since her mum had discovered who her 'beau' was, there'd been doubt.

Would the same thing happen with Anthony's family? Would his mother be suspicious of him dating a mere nurse? Would she think of her as a possible gold-digger? A fake? They needed this thing to seem real to everyone else—which meant that a phone call telling someone she was dating was utterly different from *showing* people that they were dating. She could picture holding his hand. She could imagine dancing with him on the dance floor. But could she see herself kissing him? Being affectionate with him?

He was handsome, sure. Attractive, most definitely. And maybe if he'd been a perfect stranger and they hadn't had the history they had with one another, then, hell, yeah, she'd have noticed him in a bar. Maybe flirted a little.

But they did know one another. And that changed things.

It'll be okay. He's not looking for anything and neither am I.

She felt bad about lying to people, but who was it hurting? No one. It would make both their parents happy, their wider circle happy, and it would make *them* happy because everyone would finally be off their backs. There was no downside to it.

He was a friend—and besides, she really wanted to experience a little more of his life. Peep behind the curtain and see the Duke of Weston. Who wouldn't be curious? Seeing how the other half lived. How *he* lived. Since running into him again and getting to know him she'd been able to feel herself being drawn into his orbit.

Julia stood and unzipped the cover on her dress. Her fingers trailed down the soft pink silk and tulle as she imagined herself in it. Swirling around the dance floor in Anthony's arms with everyone watching. It was every little girl's dream to be the belle of the ball, and here was her opportunity. It was going to be amazing. And all she had to do to enjoy it was to relax into the idea and just accept it.

She started on her hair first. She liked the way Celine had twisted her hair up in the boutique and left little waves hanging, so once she'd washed and dried it she used a hot iron to add curls to the soft tendrils after she'd pinned up the rest of it with diamante hair slides. She kept her make-up minimal, creating a soft, smoky eye and a nude lip, and once she'd found the perfect underwear that would not show or ruin the line of the dress she slid into the ballgown, strapped on the heels and stood in front of the mirror to check her reflection.

I look like a fairytale princess.

She couldn't help but smile, and then laugh with delight. At heart, Julia was a romantic, and she'd grown up like most little girls reading stories about princesses who met handsome princes or were saved from dragons by knights, who whisked them away to their palaces for a happy-ever-after. And though Anthony was no prince, and he didn't have a palace, he was a duke, and he had a duchy, and he was going to dance with her at the ball and pretend to be in love with her. They would twirl and whirl around the ballroom, staring into each other's eyes, and...

And *nothing*.

She would not let herself be carried away by the fairytale. Life so far had proved to her that fairytales were nothing but myths. All she'd ever attracted were frogs.

A knock at her door had her gaze rushing to the clock. It was seven-thirty on the dot. Anthony was right on time.

She checked her hair and make-up one final time, then glided to the door and opened it.

Anthony stood outside, looking like the perfect gentleman. He wore a tuxedo, but instead of a black bow tie he wore one in soft blush-pink. Even his pocket square was the same colour, to match her gown. The suit clung in all the right places and in one hand he held a single red rose, which he proffered to her. In the other, he held two velvet-lined boxes.

Julia smiled and took the rose, pressing it to her nose to inhale the scent. It was long-stemmed and thorn-free, and its rich aroma filled her nose with a warm deliciousness that only roses could.

'Thank you. It's beautiful.'

'Not as beautiful as you.'

She blushed, feeling ridiculously pleased by his words, her stomach doing somersaults.

'There's no one here to hear that. Save your compliments for when we're there.'

But she liked it that he'd said it anyway. Almost as if he meant it.

He smiled. 'I have two other things for you.'

'Oh?'

He tilted his head. 'May I come in?'

'Of course!' She stepped back, closing the door behind him as he made her turn and face the hall mirror.

'Close your eyes.'

She felt excited. As if her whole body was humming with anticipation and thrill. She closed her eyes and listened intently. Heard him open one of the boxes. And then there was nothing—until she felt him drape something cold around her neck, fastening a clasp at the back.

'Open your eyes.'

Was this really happening? Smiling, she opened her eyes and then gasped out loud at the sight of the beautiful ruby and diamond teardrop necklace that he had placed around her neck. Set in gold, it glimmered and gleamed, catching the light as she moved.

'Anthony! This is…beautiful! Where did you get it?'

'It's been in the family for a while. It's nothing.'

'Nothing?' She wanted to touch it, but was almost afraid to. She could feel its weight, its history, its worth around her neck, but still she wanted to reassure herself that it was actually there.

'And these to match.'

He passed her the second, smaller box, and she opened it up to reveal ruby and diamond teardrop earrings.

'Oh, my gosh!'

'I thought they would look perfect with your dress. I hope you don't mind?'

'Mind?' Of course she didn't mind! She couldn't believe it. Never in her wildest dreams would she ever have thought that something like this could happen to her. 'Anthony, this is amazing. Thank you.'

'I just knew you'd look perfect in them.'

He stood behind her right shoulder, looking into the mirror at her. Admiring her. Smiling as if he was really happy. And she was, too.

'It will really help with our ruse if you're wearing the family jewellery.'

Of course. The *ruse*. She'd forgotten that for a moment, so caught up had she been in the fantasy. The disappointment she felt was sickening, but she reminded herself quickly that this was what it was all about. Being convincing to his family as well as hers. And this was what it would take to convince them.

'They know you're bringing me?' she asked.

'I've told them that I've been seeing someone quietly, yes. That I wanted to keep you to myself for a while. You know…like a good boyfriend would.'

'Of course.'

But she didn't want to be hidden. She wanted to

think of him as shouting about her from the rooftops. Even if this was fake, she wanted that. To feel special.

'We should get going then, shouldn't we?' she said.

He checked his watch. 'Yes. I have a car waiting for us downstairs.'

He had a car waiting?

Anthony gave her his arm as they left her flat and she stepped outside to see a sleek, dark saloon car, with a chauffeur standing by the open rear passenger door. A *chauffeur*!

'Evening, ma'am,' said the man in a grey uniform and hat.

'Good evening. What's your name?'

'Mason, ma'am.'

She smiled. 'Thank you, Mason. Call me Julia.'

'Yes, ma'am.' He bowed.

Anthony caught her gaze and smiled at her.

Was this how the other half lived? Looked after? Served by staff? And yet Anthony worked. He worked hard. He wasn't waited on at the hospital. He had clearly gone looking for something fulfilling in life. He didn't just want *easy*. She admired him for that.

He took her hand as she got into the car. Helped her with her skirts as she sat down. Mason closed the door and Anthony got in the other side.

'Ready for this?'

'As I'll ever be. What does everyone know about me? What have you told them?'

'Your name.'

'That's it?'

'Like I said—I told them I wanted to keep you to myself for a little while. I've said they can ask you all the questions they want when they meet you.'

'And what do I say?'

'Tell them the truth.'

'That I'm a nurse?'

He smiled at her. 'Yes.'

'But won't they be expecting someone...*more* than that?'

'That's on them. Lying would make this more complicated than it needs to be. Let's just look like two people who are enjoying each other's company. We're still dating, remember? Still getting to know one another. Finding out how we might fit in with each other's family and friends.'

'And this is me making my debut?'

'Yes.'

'And doing it in style!'

He laughed. 'Yes! Are you nervous? Is there anything I can do to make this easier for you?'

As they drove through the city she looked out of the window at the ordinary people just walking by, getting on with their lives. Maybe coming home from work or going out for the evening to the local pub. And here she was, dressed up like a princess, in a chauffeur-driven car, about to be presented to dukes and earls and God only knew who else.

'Stay close?' she said.

Anthony smiled. 'I can do that.'

It took about an hour for them to drive out of town and reach the countryside where the manor was. Weston House looked imposing and regal, with a crenellated roof, a long sweeping driveway and high columns by the front door, where a butler waited with a tray of champagne to greet the guests.

The car swept right up to the doors and Mason got out and opened her door, standing back so that Anthony could take her hand and help her alight from the car.

Her stomach was filled with butterflies and she felt incredibly excited as well as nervous. Would her legs hold her up? They felt trembly. Weak. But as she took Anthony's hand and he slipped her arm through his, all the while smiling at her, she felt a strength begin to grow inside her. The feeling that with him on her arm she could do this.

Julia smiled back and even laughed a little.

'Your Grace…'

The butler nodded as they passed and stepped into a vast entryway that almost had Julia gaping. Twin staircases swept up on either side and the walls were covered in portraits of stern-faced men and imperious-looking women dressed in their finery, each one with a small brass plaque beneath, giving their name. The floor was marble, and over in one corner something caught her eye.

'Is that a suit of armour?'

Anthony nodded. 'Yes, actually, it is.'

'You have a *suit of armour*?' she asked again, just to clarify.

'I do.'

'Have you ever worn it?'

He laughed. 'No.'

'Maybe you should?'

She turned and winked at him, but he simply smiled and guided her towards the room where the music was coming from. It sounded as if an actual orchestra was playing, but she wasn't sure it was a real one until they got to the double doors of the ballroom and she saw the twelve-piece orchestra situated on a raised dais over to their left.

'His Grace the Duke of Weston and Miss Julia Morris!'

She'd not expected to be announced. Julia had kind of hoped that they would just enter the room and slowly mingle, and she would get to know everyone one by one, but suddenly all heads turned and she felt the gaze of *every single person* in the room.

Oh, my God. What are we doing?

Her smile was frozen to her face and her hand clutched Anthony's arm tightly, but he was moving forward and she had no choice but to step with him as he walked her right onto the dance floor.

'Relax,' he told her.

'People are looking.'

'Of course they are. They're intrigued. I've not brought a date to any social event in the last ten years.'

'What if they hate me?'

'That's their issue, not ours.'

'But what if they tell me to my face?'

'People aren't that rude.'

'Clearly you never went to my kind of school.'

He looked at her then. Raised an eyebrow. 'People told you they hated you?'

'Shelly Radcliffe did. She hated me. Because I got to sit next to Danny Howard and he was my dance partner.'

'How old were you?'

'Ten.'

He smirked. 'Years ago. Kids can be brutally honest. Thankfully, we adults hide behind etiquette and masks.'

'So you're saying they might hate me, but they'll keep it to themselves?'

'Or gossip about you with their friends—but never to your face.'

'Oh, well, that's okay, then,' she replied sarcastically.

'Relax. I'll keep you safe. Just keep looking into my eyes.'

She could do that.

Anthony began to twirl her around the dance

floor. A waltz was playing and she tried to focus on her footwork and looking graceful, knowing that if she made a single mistake, like stepping on his foot or stumbling, then everyone would notice.

She had to be perfect.

For the next few hours and the next six weeks, until his mother went to Australia, she had to be perfect girlfriend material.

How hard could it possibly be?

CHAPTER SIX

As HE'D EXPECTED, all eyes were on them. He saw questions in the eyes of many ladies. A raised eyebrow on the face of the Duchess of Denby. Even open jealousy on the face of Lady Annabella, whom he'd been forced to endure a lunch with two weeks ago—thanks, once again, to his mother.

But on his mother's face he saw a smile. Approval. Intrigue. He knew it must be killing her to wait whilst they danced, knew that she would want to take Julia aside and talk to her, ask questions and delve into her life like a bloodhound.

Well, she would have to wait. Because for now he was dancing with his beautifully stunning girlfriend. Dancing with a woman he was proud to be with and experiencing feelings and thoughts that he'd never expected to feel when he'd suggested this ruse.

He felt as if he'd won already. Outsmarting his mother. Letting Lady Annabella know that she was not his choice without saying so outright and hurting her feelings. And here he was. Dancing. With Julia in his arms. And it couldn't have felt easier.

He felt so comfortable with her. Maybe it was because they'd been bound together by that fateful night ten years ago? Whatever it was, he felt as if he could share anything with her and it would be all right. That she would keep any secrets if he needed. This ease he felt, though, he had to admit was slightly alarming. Unexpected. Concerning. He'd never thought he'd ever feel this way again. Protective. *Attached.*

By coming here with him she'd made herself a small fish swimming in a shark tank, and yet she didn't look perturbed at all. There was a sparkle in Julia's eyes. She looked happy. And he liked it that she was happy.

'How are you doing?' he whispered.

'All right. The dancing helps. Means I only have to look at you and not at everyone else.' She paused. 'Are they all still staring at us?'

He smiled back. 'Yes. Shall we give them a show?'

A wicked gleam entered her eyes. 'Lead the way.'

Smirking, he led them into a series of twirls and spins that caused her beautiful skirts to billow out around her. Clockwise. Anti-clockwise. They took up the whole floor. He worried that he might be making her feel dizzy, but she kept step with him and he saw the challenge in her eyes, felt the knowledge that anything he did she would be able to match.

As the music built towards its end he moved them to the centre of the dance floor and performed a standing spin, a ronde, a contra check, and then moved into another turn. But instead of looking past his shoulder Julia stared into his eyes, and he was hypnotised into looking back into hers. They were keeping each other strong, keeping each other safe…

When the music ended, the bubble was broken by the arrival of his sister Zoey. And he was grateful for the interruption. Because he could only stare into Julia's beautiful doe-like eyes for a moment and he was lost in them. And he didn't like feeling lost.

'Anthony! You really know how to put on a show… And here was me thinking that you were the family wallflower. Are you going to introduce me to this stunning woman who has finally brought you out of your shell?'

Zoey wore a royal blue dress, off the shoulder, and now she turned to gaze at Julia with a large, friendly smile.

'This is Julia. Julia—my sister Zoey.' He paused. 'She doesn't normally bite.'

Julia smiled. 'Pleased to meet you, Zoey.'

Zoey leaned in. 'Lady Annabella and our mother are on the prowl, so if you don't want to be gored by lionesses right away I can smuggle you into a corner where you can at least get a glass of champagne down you to fortify yourselves.'

'Oh, I'm sure they're not that bad,' Julia said.

Zoey raised an eyebrow and stared at him. 'Did you tell her nothing before tonight? Come on.'

Anthony followed as Zoey led them over to a corner behind the orchestra, catching the attention of a member of staff and asking him to bring them three flutes of champagne.

Once they possessed drinks, Zoey turned to talk to Julia once again. 'Your dress is stunning!'

'Thank you. I love yours, too.'

'This old thing? I wore it to the evening do of some politician's wedding.'

'Well, it's gorgeous,' Julia said.

'Oh, I love her already, Anthony. So, tell me… how did you two meet? Everyone is agog at the news that my dear, tragically single brother has finally found himself someone new.'

'We met at work.'

'You're a doctor?' interrupted a new, imperious voice before Julia could answer.

Anthony turned to greet his mother, whom he kissed on both cheeks. 'Evening, Mother.'

'Hello, dear. Zoey. Did you two really think you could hide away here? I've had years' worth of practice in knowing your hiding places.' She smiled at them both, letting them know that she could easily outwit them. 'Julia! How lovely to meet you at last.'

'Julia, this is my mother, the Dowager Duchess of Weston.'

'Your Grace…' Julia gave a small curtsey.

'My son has told me barely anything about you. And now, after that display on the dance floor, you'll be needing a long rest. Come with me and tell me all about yourself.'

He did not want his mother to monopolise her, or tear her from his grasp. 'I was about to give Julia the tour,' he said.

'Well, can't that wait? People are here to see *you*, darling.'

'No, they're here to raise money for charity.'

'I'm not a doctor,' Julia interjected, perhaps sensing an impending argument. 'I'm a nurse. A newly qualified nurse, actually. I work on the orthopaedic ward in the same hospital as Anthony.'

'Oh! But Anthony has always been against relationships forming in the workplace.'

Julia slid her fingers into his and looked up at him with a genuine heartfelt smile. 'Well, I guess when you know, you know.'

His mother looked from Julia to him and then back again. Considering. Weighing. 'What were you before you qualified as a nurse?'

'A waitress in a café.'

His mother smiled. 'Your life has changed dramatically, then?'

'Ever since starting at the hospital, yes.'

Anthony felt the warmth in Julia's smile as she

gazed at him. Felt the squeeze of her fingers in his. Saw that she was totally assured in the face of his mother. He admired her for that.

'My son is a prime catch. What was it about him that made you interested?'

'His kindness. The welcome he gave me. His care and attention. The look in his eyes when he speaks to me. The way he makes me feel when I'm with him.'

Anthony looked at Julia, smiling broadly. Every word she spoke was truthful, even though this relationship was a lie. Nobody here would be able to pick it apart. By having Julia at his side he was a different man. It was as if he could feel himself coming back to life, unaware that he'd been drifting for so long. *Her* kindness, *her* welcome, *her* care and attention... She made him feel *alive*.

'She's going to make my head swell,' he said now. 'Julia, you remember I promised to show you the library?'

She nodded.

'Excuse us.' He draped Julia's hand over his arm and led her away. 'Well done,' he said quietly. 'Not everyone can stand up to my mother's interrogations.'

'She wasn't that bad. She's just looking out for you. She loves you and wants the best person for you. There's nothing wrong in that.'

'I know. I just sometimes disagree with her methods.'

'I like your sister.'

'Zoey? Yeah, she's good. She was my rock when Yael died. Came and called on me every day to make sure I was okay. Got me out for a walk around the grounds even when I didn't want to do anything.'

'It's good to have people like that in your corner. You have a strong, accomplished family. Maybe you should let them in more?'

He laughed. 'I must tell my mother you said that.'

'Why?'

'She'll love you for ever.'

Julia chuckled as he led her up a staircase and down a red-carpeted hallway hung with drapes and tapestries towards the library, his pride and joy. He hadn't promised to show her anything. The lie about showing her the library had simply slipped from his lips. It was really his desire to be alone. He'd never been fond of these big, social gatherings, and as an introvert he would often slip away to recharge his social battery. Tonight, the thought of being alone with Julia was overwhelming. He wanted a moment with her. A moment to breathe and gather himself.

As they reached the library he swung open the doors with a sigh of relief, stepping to one side to allow Julia a moment of seeing it. He knew it was grand. Impressive. He'd collected a lot of the books himself. Finding first editions of all his favourites. Amassing those that were rare. Signed editions. Folios. The most delicate were kept in sealed glass cases, away from dust and light. The carpet was a rich moss-green, the drapes a forest-green. The tall windows usually let in beams of sunlight to brighten the soft recliners, the comfortable chairs adorned with cushions embroidered with hares and stags. The library was his retreat.

'Anthony! This is…' Her voice trailed off in awe as she walked past a shelf, her fingertips trailing over the books.

'I know.'

'Have you read all of these?'

'As many as I possibly could. Perhaps thirty per cent are still unread. Do you like books?'

'Are you kidding me? They're my happy place.'

He smiled at that. Glad. Because they were his happy place, too. 'Good.'

She slid a book from the shelf and flicked through it. An eighteenth-century text adorned with drawings of botanicals. She marvelled at each sketch. 'Can we stay in here all night, instead?' she asked.

Anthony laughed. 'Unfortunately our presence will be required downstairs. The revelation that you used to be a waitress will be all around the ball-room by now.'

'Should I not have said it?' She turned to him, concern in her gaze.

'Of course you should! There is nothing wrong with being a waitress.'

'But a waitress who has nabbed a duke? That might not be going down very well.'

'I don't care what they think. I've never let their thoughts and opinions on such matters interfere with my life before. Yael was a cook.'

She smiled. 'Really? She was? That's good to know. I'd hate to think you were a snob. Especially since I'm going out with you.' She winked at him, and then he saw her notice that the book she held had an inscription: *With love, Yael x.*

She slid the book back upon the shelf. 'You must miss her so much…'

He nodded. 'Things happen every day that I think she would love to hear about. Sometimes I talk to her out loud. I've told her about meeting up with you again.'

'And what did she say?'

Julia came towards him, her skirts grazing the carpet as if she were walking through a forest.

'She was happy.'

'Good.'

She reached for his hand and held it in hers. Her soft touch was alluring. The comfort it brought made him realise just how much he'd missed that kind of casual touch.

'Well?' she said. 'Should we descend upon the masses once again? Show them my robot?'

She began making robotic dance moves, and in her elegant dress she made even that look amazing. He laughed, surprised at the way she could make him smile, but knew that they couldn't hide out here for ever.

'Sure. Let's surprise them even more.'

Julia giggled. 'Maybe I should keep that special dance move for your eyes only?'

'All right. If you say so. Come on. We'd better get back downstairs in time for the auction.'

'Lead on, my love.'

She slipped her arm into his and he led them both back towards the ballroom.

CHAPTER SEVEN

THE BALL HAD been a complete success, in Julia's eyes.

It had raised money for charity, Anthony had only had to dance with her, and his mother had had no reason to introduce him to any eligible young women—although Lady Annabella had looked particularly sour-faced and cheated.

She'd even made a new friend in Zoey, who'd given her her mobile phone number and promised to ring and arrange a meet-up for coffee. She sensed that Zoey could become a great friend, but knew that friendship would be threatened by their subterfuge. Guilt made her wonder if Zoey would still want to know her after the fake relationship with her brother was over...

'Did you have a good time?' he asked now.

'Despite the guilt? Amazing, thank you.'

'Not too stressful?'

'Actually, no. It went easier than I thought. People seemed to believe we're really into one another.'

'Yes.' He gave a small laugh and glanced out of

the window before turning back to look at her. 'You know, if I haven't already said thank you for all of this, then I want to say it now. This may seem like a silly thing we're doing, but it means a lot to me. That you're willing to help me with this.'

'Hey, you're doing the same thing for me.'

'True. Do you have any family events coming up that maybe I ought to accompany you to?'

'My grandmother is having her eightieth birthday party a week tomorrow.'

'Next Sunday?'

She nodded. Her Gramma May was her only living grandparent, and she meant the world to her.

'I can make that, if you'd like me to come along?'

'It won't be as grand as your ball. It'll just be a small get-together in a council house. Sausages on sticks and trifle in the fridge…that kind of thing.'

'I love trifle.' He smiled.

Julia laughed. 'Okay! It's a date. No tux, though. Just casual.'

'You say that like I don't have any casual clothes.'

'I've only ever seen you in a suit!'

'And scrubs.'

'Well, yes, but they're work clothes. *Your* clothes look like they're all bespoke…made just for you.'

He looked embarrassed.

'Oh, my God, they are, aren't they?'

She laughed out loud and he began to laugh with her.

'I'll go and buy some jeans. Or some jogging bottoms.'

'And trainers—don't forget the trainers,' she joked.

'Yes, ma'am.'

He really was ridiculous! But lovely. Their worlds were so far apart, but she liked it that she could still reach him. That he was easy to be with. But she'd felt that way with Jake, too, at the beginning. And look at how that had ended up.

As Mason pulled the car up in front of her home she turned to look at Anthony. 'I really have had a wonderful night, tonight. Thank you. And thank you for this dress.'

'You're welcome.'

'I should give you these back.'

She began to remove the earrings and the necklace. She knew they weren't hers to keep. She'd just borrowed them for the night. For the ruse. But as she removed each piece she began to feel as if she was breaking their connection. Bursting the bubble. But still, it was important to be realistic, right? None of this was real, no matter how much she'd enjoyed it. Time to face reality, even if she wanted to hold on to the fairytale for a little bit longer. To feel special again.

Anthony almost looked reluctant to take them back, but he did so, laying them out in their velvet-lined boxes and staring at them glittering in the light from the street lamps overhead.

'You looked beautiful in them,' he said.

'Thank you. I felt beautiful.'

Mason opened the car door and she got out, fumbling in her small clutch bag for the keys to her flat.

Behind her, she heard Anthony get out, too. He stood behind her, as if he was guarding her, making sure she would get inside safely.

'You know that you don't need jewels to look beautiful. You were stunning without them.'

It meant *so much* that he thought that. For too long she'd felt like an afterthought. Second best. Not someone's first choice. 'You're very kind to say so.'

'It's the truth.' He shrugged and turned to look at Mason. 'Could we have a moment?'

'Of course, Your Grace.' Mason went back to the driver's side of the car and got in.

'May I kiss you goodnight?'

Julia's heart rate suddenly galloped ahead and she gave a nervous laugh. 'I guess…'

'I'm going to need a firm yes or a no.' He smiled, hands in his pockets.

A kiss goodnight? For whose sake? His family weren't around. Nor were her own. Mason would have heard them talking in the car, and surely knew about their secret, but as a member of Anthony's staff would keep his mouth shut in loyalty to his boss. And did he mean a kiss on the cheek? Or on the mouth? She'd not kissed him at all tonight at the ball. She'd held his hand, slipped her arm through this, smiled sweetly at him and gazed lovingly into his eyes.

But kiss him?

She had to admit, if she was being honest, that the idea not only excited her, but terrified her. None of this was real and yet…part of her wanted it to be. Part of her wanted him to yearn to kiss her. And those feelings were terrifying and thrilling in the extreme.

Cheeks burning, she gazed up at him softly. 'Yes, you may.'

Her heart pounded in her chest as he leaned towards her. Her breath was catching in her throat, her skin seemed alive, feeling every breath of wind that grazed her. Her senses went into overdrive as his face grew closer and closer. It was as if she could hear the hum of the streetlight above, could taste the aroma of fish and chips in the air from the takeout shop at the end of her road, could smell Anthony's cologne as he leaned in…

At the last minute his lips brushed her cheek and she closed her eyes to capture the moment.

And then it was done.

He was pulling back, smiling, walking away to the car, opening the door. 'Get inside, so I know you're safe.'

She nodded, blushing, glad of the darkness so he wouldn't be able to see the flush on her face. And then her hands were fumbling for her keys, and somehow she got the key into the lock without dropping them. She pushed open the door.

Had she wanted him to kiss her on the lips? Why? She reminded herself, cursing inwardly, that this wasn't real and she didn't need the complication of actually falling for him…

'See you at work on Monday,' he said.

'Yes. You too.'

Julia gave a wave and closed the door, locking it behind her, then frowned at herself. She groaned and headed up the stairs to get out of the dress and the heels and slip into something a little more comfortable.

Anthony couldn't wait to get into work on Monday morning. He felt light, happy—and, weirdly enough, when his mother had called to speak to him on Sunday, she'd told him that she liked Julia. That she seemed like a good fit for him—which had been surprising, but welcome.

He and Julia had certainly put on a show, and to be fair, his partner in crime had made it very easy indeed. The guilt he'd initially felt about fooling everyone had simply died when he'd walked into that ballroom with Julia dazzling in her gorgeous dress. Even Annabella's sour face hadn't ruined it. And the evening itself had been very successful—not just for him, but also for the charity, raising thousands of pounds.

He couldn't wait to see Julia again. Couldn't wait

to see her smile and hear her voice and just be near her again. She'd made him feel so good. So relaxed. So happy. It had been a long time since he'd felt like that and it was all down to her. He knew he needed to rein his feelings in. Become Mr Ice again as he entered the walls of the hospital. But it was difficult when he felt so light. So free. These feelings she engendered within him were dizzying.

When he walked onto the ward and found her in the supplies room, collecting some dressings for a bandage change, a broad smile broke across his face. 'Good morning!'

'Morning!' she replied.

'How are you?' he asked.

'Great! You?'

'Amazing. Just thought I'd check in with you before I start my rounds.'

'Oh, okay. I'm just getting dressings for Mr Bundy's leg. He's soaked through them.'

'All right. Do you fancy meeting up later? For lunch in the cafeteria? Start the rumours here?'

She looked around them. 'Actually, like I said before, if you don't mind…can we *not* be in a relationship here at work? This is my first job as a nurse, and I don't really want people gossiping about me here and thinking that I'm anything other than good at my job. Is that okay?'

He'd not thought about that, and instantly felt subdued. 'Of course. You're right. I can continue to be Mr Ice here, at least.'

'You don't mind?'

'No. Of course not. Okay, well… I'll see you around.'

She smiled at him. 'You will.'

He left the room, cursing himself inwardly for not even thinking about her reputation here. Of course she would want everyone here on the ward and in this hospital to recognise that she was earnest and hardworking and good at her job, and not just here to bag a doctor. A lot of people assumed that about nurses—wrongly—just perpetuating a stereotype. She was right to say what she had and he admired her for that.

They needed to be sensible about this and not get carried away. This was where they both worked, and when this was all over they would still have to work together. Wouldn't that be easier if they didn't have to pretend to avoid each other after the 'break-up'?

Perhaps work was where they shouldn't pretend? Where they were just who they were?

And so he made his way through his rounds, behaving as he normally would, but he couldn't help but notice whenever Julia was around. It was as if his gaze was pulled towards her, like a moth hypnotised by a flame.

He didn't question it. He didn't worry about it. Supposed it was natural after having spent some time together. Since she'd been on his arm in front of his family.

Because they were friends.

Partners.

He was extremely fond of her, and perhaps he was even feeling a little more than that—but it was only natural, considering how close they'd had to be. She was probably the only person in this whole hospital that he *was* fond of. Yes, he had colleagues. Acquaintances. Other surgeons he occasionally met up with to play golf, or have drinks at some kind of function. He was friendly with them, but would he confide in them? No.

I could with Julia, he thought. *In fact, I do already.*

But that reminded him that he also needed to keep her at arm's length, and that was welcome.

No point in getting carried away in their fiction.

CHAPTER EIGHT

How COULD A guy who looked so devastatingly handsome in a suit or a tuxedo look just as amazing in a distressed pair of jeans and a fitted black tee shirt?

When Julia opened her front door, she literally gasped. 'Oh, my God.'

Anthony looked down at himself, alarmed. 'Is it too casual?'

'No! No, it's…perfect,' she said, trying not to smile at the wave of attraction she felt for him.

This guy was hitting it out of the park, without even trying that hard! How could it be that, seeing him in tee shirt and jeans, she was more aware of every muscle he had? How broad those shoulders of his were… How his forearms—God, those forearms!—looked so fabulously sexy?

'I didn't know what to get your grandmother, so I did a little digging from the information that you've given me and I've paid for her to have a treatment day at her local salon. Hair, make-up, manicure, pedicure… Too much, or not enough?'

He genuinely looked unsure.

She laughed. 'Well, you've never met her before—she's a total stranger to you. So…yeah, that might be construed as a little bit too much. You could just buy her flowers?'

'Flowers. Right… We can buy some on the way.'

'But a *small* bouquet—not the entire shop. Or franchise.'

'Perfect.'

'What are you like?' She laughed again as she locked the door behind her and glanced out at his car. 'No chauffeur today?'

'Occasionally I drive myself, you know.'

'Good to know.'

She stood back as he opened the car door for her and then slid inside and waited for him to walk around and get in the driver's seat. As they drove out of London she reflected on their past week at work.

He'd kept his word and maintained his Mr Ice persona in front of other members of staff, but when they'd found themselves alone, his smiles and his inherent warmth had emerged, just for her. His friendship meant a lot to her, and she kind of liked it that they had this shared secret. This private agreement between them. When their gazes met, their shared secret felt like a small blaze inside her chest and she almost beamed with it.

As they pulled up outside a flower shop near her

mother's house, she turned to ask him a question. 'Have you ever been to a float parade?'

'A float parade? No.'

'A street parade? Mardi Gras?'

'No.' He shook his head.

'There's one being held here this year. Some of my friends are making a float from scratch. The theme is heroes and heroines, and someone's got an old flatbed truck we can use. I said I'd help out. There's a prize for best float. Do you want to join us?'

'What would it involve?'

She shrugged. 'I don't know… Making things. Painting. Decorating. Building. It's all for a good cause, too. When you go through the streets people walk alongside with buckets and collecting tins.'

'Sure. Sounds fun. Just let me know where and when.' He smiled and looked at her. 'Are you going to be on the float?'

'Oh! No. I did that last year. The theme was animals and I wore a bird costume for the whole day… I've never sweated so much in my entire life. No, this year I'll be there with my collecting tin and that's all.'

'You? A bird?'

'My mum tried to set me up with a guy dressed like a parrot. Said we looked like a pair of lovebirds—can you believe it?'

He smiled. 'What would we do without our mothers?'

'Live peaceful lives?'

Anthony laughed as they stepped into the shop. 'We'd miss them. Even though she can poke her nose in where it's not wanted, I'm still going to miss mine when she goes to Adelaide.'

'How long will she be gone for?'

'Two months. What about those?' He pointed at a bucket holding miniature bouquets.

'Perfect.'

They pulled up in front of an ordinary terraced council house with a neat front garden. A small, square lawn. One flowerbed filled with roses. A pot with a dwarf fern in it either side of the front door, which was painted dark blue.

Julia rang the doorbell.

'When was the last time you saw your grandma?' he asked.

'Just before I started at the hospital.'

The door was opened by a woman who looked like the older version of Julia. Her hair was dark brown too, but shoulder-length and there was a grey streak at the front. Her smile was the same as Julia's and she greeted him with huge warmth.

'You must be Anthony! I've heard so much about you!' Unexpectedly she threw her arms around him and hugged him close, whispering, 'I've wanted to thank you for a very long time. For looking after my girl that night. And for Marcus.'

Julia had told him that her mother knew he was

the same Anthony who had delivered Marcus, but that was all she had told her.

'Nice to meet you, Mrs Morris.'

'Georgia, please. Come in! Everyone else is here.'

He stepped into a room overflowing with people. At the heart of it was a little old lady, with silver hair and the same brown eyes as Georgia and Julia, sitting with balloons attached to the back of her chair.

'Gramma May! Happy Birthday!' Julia stooped down to give her gran a hug and a kiss and then stepped back. It was his turn.

'Hi. I'm Anthony. Happy Birthday.' He smiled at the older lady and passed her the bouquet.

'Roses! My favourite! How did you know?'

He looked at Julia. 'A little birdie might have told me.'

'Someone find chairs for these two,' said May.

Chairs were acquired and the three of them settled down together. Anthony had Julia to his left and Georgia to his right. He reached for Julia's hand to hold it. It felt easy, now he had already danced with her at his ball and held her close And it felt good to be touching her again. He saw the way she looked at him and smiled as he did so. Was she enjoying it, too?

'Would you like a drink?' Julia asked.

'Whatever you're having will be fine.'

'Won't be a minute.'

She released him and got up and headed into the kitchen.

'I've heard so much about you, of course.' Georgia leaned in when her daughter was gone. 'The way you helped my daughter that night… How you delivered Marcus… I've never been so grateful to a stranger in my entire life.'

'Anyone would have done the same.'

'I hope so. But she was lucky to find you and your lovely wife. I was so sorry to hear of her passing.'

'Thank you. And I was devastated to learn of Marcus's.'

'It was a very difficult time for us all, as I'm sure you can imagine. Well… You know grief, too.'

'Too much.'

He didn't like to remember those dark days after Yael's death. They'd been hard enough to live through. He didn't need to keep bringing them out and re-examining them. Why would he torture himself like that?

'So, to learn that you two were dating…' Georgia went on. 'Well, I was taken aback, at first, if I'm honest. But I've had time to think about it and it's nice to know that Julia's with a real man. The kind of man who can step up to the plate and be strong, you know? Be honest with her. She's been lied to enough, what with all that business with Jake, Marcus's father. Not that he deserves that title.'

Anthony would never want to lie to Julia. He would never want to hurt her.

'I'm an honest man. At least, I hope I am.'

'Good. I'm glad to hear it. I've worried about her being alone all this time. Oh, she'd hate knowing that I'm saying all of this to you, but she's my daughter, and I love her, and she's been through enough torment in her life. I only want to see her happy and no longer alone.'

'I understand. My mother feels the same way about me.'

'Your mother and I would get along perfectly, then!' Georgia smiled.

'I'm sure you would.'

He could just imagine Georgia and his mother sitting at high tea, china cups in their hands as they discussed their children. They'd get along very well.

Julia arrived back then, with drinks, passing him orange juice in a glass, with ice. 'What are you two talking about?'

'You, of course!' Georgia laughed.

Anthony tried to keep up with all the different conversations going on in the room, but everyone was talking to each other at once so he sat and listened politely. Everyone was reminiscing. Recalling Gramma May stories. It sounded as if she was a really cool grandma, which was great. He had no memories of grandparents himself. They had died when he was very young. There were portraits on the wall, and occasionally his mother would mention her parents fondly, but she found it difficult to speak of them, so he never asked. It was the same thing with his dad. He'd died shortly after Anthony was born. Helicopter crash.

'I remember when Georgia came to visit and brought her new husband with her. I never much liked him,' Gramma May said. 'He seemed a little full of himself to me. Remember I told you that you were expecting, Georgia? You didn't even know you were carrying Julia.'

Georgia nodded. 'I remember.'

'And do you remember me telling you that you had nine months to sort that man out or he wouldn't stick around?'

'Yes, we all remember, Mum.'

'And I was right. He buggered off. Stayed for the cute stage…disappeared as soon as she hit the terrible twos.' Gramma May rubbed at her forehead as if she had pain or discomfort there. 'I remember s-s-saying to you…you look after that little…' Her voice trailed off as if she couldn't quite think of the word.

Girl. That was what she meant to say, Anthony knew, but his red flags had gone up. Was this just a normal glitch in an octogenarian's memory, or something more sinister happening before their very eyes?

'Gramma May?' Julia was frowning.

'I… I'm…'

And then he saw it. The droop to her face. She

was trying to smile, but it was only happening on one side.

Both he and Julia rushed to their feet at the same time.

She had seen it too, for what it was.

Gramma May was having a stroke, right before their eyes.

'Somebody call for an ambulance,' Anthony instructed calmly, turning to look Georgia directly in the eyes.

'Why? What's happening?'

'I think your mother is having a stroke.'

'What? Mum?'

'Mum!' Julia interrupted. 'Call for an ambulance, now!'

Anthony knelt before Gramma May, and with a smile and in a kind voice asked her to smile. It was still lopsided. He asked her to repeat a sentence that he gave her. Her speech was slurred and her words incomplete. He asked her to try and raise her arms in front of her with her eyes closed, and although she could move both arms, one rose higher than the other.

He turned to Georgia, who was on the phone with the emergency services. 'Please tell them that she has a positive FAST test.'

Georgia nodded as Julia asked everyone, even though they were concerned, to stand back and give Gramma May some room to breathe.

He did not know what was going on in her brain.

It could be a burst blood vessel, or a clot. There was nothing he could do but remain calm.

'We should give her aspirin or something!' someone called out.

Anthony shook his head. 'No. If she has a bleed on her brain, that could make it worse.' He noted the time on his watch. They had an hour to help May. It was called the golden hour by medics because if a patient received definitive treatment within the first sixty minutes of an event then they were likely to have good results. As opposed to after that amount of time, when the risk of complications, deficits or even death might be higher.

'We have to do something!' said another voice. 'Aren't you a doctor?'

'I am. But there's nothing we can do until the paramedics arrive. Maybe someone could get her a blanket? A pillow for her head?'

Relatives rushed around trying to do something. He understood the urge. No one liked to feel helpless or impotent in the face of such upsetting events. Actually doing something, no matter how small, would help to make them feel better later. As long as there was a good result. A bad result would make them feel like they'd not done enough.

'You're doing great, May,' he said in a soothing voice, as he held the older woman's fragile, liver-spotted hand. 'Just breathe normally and soon we'll have help here, okay?'

'We've got you, Gramma May,' said Julia, helping to drape the blanket over her grandma's legs.

Gramma May looked upset. She tried to speak, but her words were still slurred and unclear. Her eyes looked frightened.

'Don't try to speak yet. Just breathe normally. We're all here for you,' he soothed.

It didn't take too long for the paramedics to arrive. About ten minutes. Anthony and Julia gave them the facts and the timing of the suspected stroke to pass along to the doctors in Emergency. The paramedics could only take one person in the ambulance with them, so Georgia went with her mother and Anthony told Julia they would follow behind in his car.

Gramma May went off with lights and sirens blaring, and Anthony and Julia left everyone else to clear up after the party as they headed off to the local hospital, promising to call the others with updates once they had them.

Anthony glanced at Julia as he drove and reached for her hand, squeezing it. 'Are you all right?' he asked. He knew what it felt like to feel as if you couldn't help a person you loved.

She nodded, biting at her bottom lip. 'She's just always been there, you know...?'

'I know.'

'She's always been a part of my life. I can't imagine her not being here.'

'She's strong.'

'Yes. I'm sure she'll get through this. The woman has nine lives! She was bombed as a child, you know, before she was evacuated out of London.'

'Yeah?'

'Yeah.' She squeezed back, gaining strength from his touch. 'She'll get through this, too. Nothing can stop her.'

'The Morris women are strong,' he said with a smile.

'We've always had to be.'

Sitting in the family room waiting for an update seemed interminable. Julia would pace for a little bit in the small area, then sit down. And then, when she got twitchy again, she would pace again.

'Do you want me to go and see if I can get an update?' Anthony asked.

'Would you?'

'Sure. Stay here a moment.'

When he was gone she began biting her nails, and she turned to look at her mum. 'Do you think Gramma May will be all right?'

'I don't know…'

'Tell me what happened again. When you arrived in the emergency department.'

'They took her off for a scan and someone brought me here. Said they'd fetch me when they could.'

'Okay.'

Julia began pacing again. She didn't like being

in this hospital. The last time she'd been here, in this A&E had been when she'd lost Marcus. And even though she knew in her heart that Marcus had actually passed away at home, his death had been confirmed *here*, so she associated this place with dying. She couldn't lose Gramma May here, too.

The door opened and Anthony was there. 'We can go and see her now,' he told them.

When they got to her bedside Gramma May still wasn't able to talk, but a doctor in green scrubs was waiting to speak to them.

'We've had the scan results back and they show a clot in May's brain. We would like your permission to administer a clot-busting drug, which should work quite quickly and hopefully restore as much function as we can.'

'Then do it,' Julia's mum said.

The doctor nodded. 'You do need to be aware, however, of the risks in taking thrombolysis medication. It can very quickly dissolve the clot, and restore blood flow to the parts of your mum's brain that have been starved of it, but we need to check some things first. Has May any history of high blood pressure?'

'No. If anything she has low blood pressure.'

'Any bleeding issues? Or a head injury?'

'No.'

'Okay. This drug can cause a bleed in the brain within seven days of being administered, so you'll need to be on the lookout for any signs of that. I'll get the rt-PA if you're happy for us to proceed with this treatment.'

Rt-PA stood for recombinant tissue plasminogen activator, and was a standard treatment for dealing with ischaemic stroke.

Georgia looked at Julia. 'We are.'

'All right.'

They watched as the drug was administered.

'How long will it take before we see results?' Julia asked.

'It can be a couple of hours—or even a couple of days in some cases. We'll keep her here for monitoring initially, and then in a few hours we'll move her up to the stroke ward.'

'Can we stay with her?'

'Of course. Can I get someone to bring you a cup of tea, or anything?'

'That's very kind. Thank you.'

'I'll get it,' Anthony said. 'You guys are rushed off your feet.'

The doctor nodded and left the bedside.

'Georgia, why don't you sit down here,' Anthony suggested. 'And I'll grab another chair for Julia.'

'You're very kind, Anthony, thank you,' Georgia said.

When Anthony had disappeared, her mother sat down on the opposite side of Gramma May's bed, looked at Julia and smiled softly. 'You've got a good one there, Jools.'

Julia nodded. 'I have.'

'Don't let him go.'

'I'll try not to.'

She didn't know what else to say. It did feel amazing to have his support. For him to be by her side during this difficult time. In this moment she felt as if maybe she ought to just tell her mother the truth about her and Anthony. Come clean. But did she really want to declare all whilst Gramma May couldn't speak? She and Anthony weren't important right now. Her grandmother was.

Anthony arrived back with another chair for her and she settled into it, and then he disappeared again to get them some drinks.

Her mum was right. He really was good. He'd only just met her family and yet here he was, taking care of them as if they were his own. Of course he was a doctor, and he knew how to speak to families who were worried and upset. He knew that they needed comfort and reassurance and he was trying to provide them with that. The way he'd taken care of May when he'd noticed the stroke happening a split second before she had had been amazing. He'd not panicked. He'd not tried to alarm anyone. He'd been calm and decisive and in charge. He'd stepped up to the plate and guided everyone, when the other guests had panicked and not known what to do.

She'd been most terribly glad that he'd been there to do that. Even though she was a qualified nurse herself, it was different when the patient was one of your own. It was harder to maintain the professional distance you used at work.

When he arrived back in the cubicle carrying a small tray of drinks, she was so thankful for him... so grateful.

She took her cup of tea with a genuine smile. 'Thank you.'

'No problem. She's still sleeping?'

'Yes.'

'Probably to be expected.'

'You don't have to stay here if you've got things to do.' Julia said, not wanting to take up his entire day. She'd only expected them to be at her grandma's house for a couple of hours, and they were way past that now.

'There's nowhere else I'd rather be,' he said, taking her hand in his.

She was confused. Was that for the benefit of her mother? Or actually for her?

Part of her—no, most of her—wanted it to be just for her. Wanted this affection not to be a ruse. Not part of the show. A boyfriend would try to comfort his girlfriend at a time like this, after all. Why couldn't she see his motivation in doing this right now? But he was a good friend. And he cared about her the way she cared about him. If this situation had been reversed she'd have been at his side, as well.

She decided that this part—him holding her hand—was real.

And it meant the world.

CHAPTER NINE

As soon as she walked onto the orthopaedic ward the next Monday, Anthony came to find her. 'How's May?'

'She's doing well. Her speech is getting better. They think she can go home soon, but they want to make sure a care package is in place.'

'Good. I'm glad to hear it. She had us all worried there for a moment.'

Us.

'How are you?' she asked. 'I'm sorry we took up most of your weekend.'

Anthony had dutifully called her every day this week, and driven her back and forth to the hospital. Sitting with her. Taking care of her. Asking her if there was anything she needed. She'd told him that he didn't have to do all that. That their pretence didn't have to go so far. Their relationship was meant to be fun pretend, not dutiful pretend. But he'd simply shaken his head and told her he was her friend, she was going through a tough time, and he would treat anyone the same.

Which was nice, but… She didn't want to be just anyone to him. She wanted—needed—to be more, and that was throwing her. Confusing her.

'I didn't mind,' he said now.

'What have you got on your list today?'

'Rounds…and then I've got a clinic.'

'No surgeries today?'

'Not unless they come through A&E. You?'

'The usual. Drugs round…dressing changes.' She shrugged.

'I'd better let you get on, then. Before Sister tells me off for delaying you. Fancy meeting for lunch?'

She did, but as she'd said before she didn't want there to be rumours about them at the hospital. 'We'd best not.'

He looked disappointed. 'Okay. Well, maybe I'll see you tonight? Let me take you out to dinner.'

'You don't have to.'

'I know. I want to. If you're free?'

'Mum's with Gramma May tonight, so…yes. Please. That'll be nice.'

'I'll book a table somewhere nice.'

Rosaria, another nurse, began to walk towards them, so Julia suddenly straightened and smiled. 'Thank you, Mr Fitzpatrick. I'll get that done right away.'

'Thank you, Nurse.'

And he walked the other way to gather his registrar and the junior doctors, and the medical students who would follow him around the ward. He cut a tall, lonely figure, but that of a man in charge. A man who knew he was valued and respected.

Had it always come so easy to him? she wondered. Was life gifted on a plate to some, while others, like herself, always had to fight for respect?

As a waitress, she'd often felt like a second-class citizen. Customers would be rude and take out their frustrations with their meals or the service on her. And as a student nurse she'd often felt that she was on the bottom rung of the ladder and that the climb ahead of her was long and difficult. Now, as a qualified nurse, she'd experienced, in these two short weeks, the way some patients would not listen to her advice, preferring to hear it from 'a proper doctor'.

The one time she'd felt powerful and respected had been when she'd given birth to Marcus. She'd been recognised as a mother, a woman who had gone through the trials of labour and then birth. She had felt accepted by her peers. By the friends that she'd made in antenatal classes.

But where were they now? They'd sent cards when Marcus had passed away. One or two had phoned to check in on her. Brought flowers. Taken her out for coffee. But had any of them kept in touch since? It was as if losing her baby had somehow singled her out. As if they didn't want to associate with her. Didn't know what to say to her. She hadn't been one of them any more, and she'd so wanted to belong somewhere—which was why her university friends had become her new friendship group.

Cesca, Yvette and Janine had welcomed her with open arms. They knew about Marcus, but it didn't change the way they felt about her.

She reached into her pocket, pulled out her mobile and texted Anthony.

Let tonight be my treat. I'll take you somewhere special. J x.

'Where are we going?' Anthony asked as he cycled alongside her that evening.

As promised, she'd decided to get him on a bike, and they'd rented a couple of the ones that were available all over the city. She'd expected a few false starts, but after an initial wobble he'd actually taken to it very quickly.

'It's a surprise,' she told him.

'I don't know of any decent restaurants down here.'

'Who said anything about a restaurant?'

She winked at him and laughed, then led him along until they turned a corner to reveal a mobile food stand. It was lit up with fairy lights and revealed a longish queue trailing around the square.

'Baked potatoes?' Anthony looked confused.

She laughed. 'It's the very best baked potato you will ever have in your entire life. Trust me!'

He looked doubtful.

Julia grinned, enjoying the look on Anthony's

face. 'Haven't you ever eaten from a food truck before?'

'Of course I have!'

'Where? When?' she asked.

He shrugged. 'Well, it might not have been a truck *per se*…more of a pop-up restaurant.'

'Serving?'

'Oysters.'

'Hah! I knew it! And I bet they cost a small fortune?'

'It was very reasonable,' he argued with a smile.

'"Reasonable" to you would probably mean a mortgage to me. Trust me—this grub you're about to eat will blow those oysters out of the water. No pun intended.'

'How wonderful can a jacket potato be?'

'Have you not seen the queue? That's how good.'

'You know I could have taken you to a wonderful little place with fine wines and a river view?'

'I don't need fine wines or a river view. Not when I can eat food out of a cardboard container whilst admiring this lovely view of a city square and a water fountain.'

'My place has a piano.'

'There's a violin player over there, busking.'

'It serves the finest spatchcock chicken you have ever seen.'

Julia shrugged. 'This has pigeons.' She laughed as she cycled through a flock of them, causing them to leap into the airs, wings flapping.

'Okay, you win.'

'I'll win once you taste the food.'

'You're promising big, Morris! This had better deliver.'

'It will!'

They parked their bikes and got into the queue. The busker was playing a recent hit from the charts and Julia found herself swaying and bopping to it, much to Anthony's amusement.

They finally reached the serving hatch.

'What can I getcha?' asked the man behind the counter.

'Do you trust me to order?' Julia asked.

'Implicitly.'

'We'll have two of your finest jacket potatoes, both with chilli beef and cheese, please.'

'Coming right up!'

The aromas from the food truck were tantalising, and after a long day at work Julia was starving and ready to eat her fill. Their food was passed over, steaming hot, and they walked over to a low stone wall, near where they'd parked their bikes, to eat with the water fountain behind them.

She could barely see the potato. It was all chilli beef and melted cheese. She dipped in her wooden fork and pulled out a forkful, watching the cheese stretching between the fork and the food in her hand before she placed it into her mouth.

'Oh, my God! Just as I remember! What do you think?'

Anthony's eyes were wide in surprise as he ate some of his own. 'I don't think I've eaten chilli this good in my entire life!'

'I told you!'

'Okay, okay. You're right. From now on, you can choose all our eateries, if their food tastes this delicious.'

'Well, I can't promise five-star food every time, but this place certainly hits the spot after a long day. How did your clinic go?'

He nodded, swallowing. 'Good. I had an interesting case come in.'

'Can you tell me about it?'

'It's a young man who's been brought over from Africa by a charity. He's had polio and his legs are malformed. We're looking to see if we can help him.'

'Really? Wow… Well, I hope you can. That could make a big difference to his quality of life.'

Anthony nodded. 'It was just an assessment today. I've arranged for up-to-date scans and we'll go from there.'

'Are his parents with him?'

'No, he's an orphan.'

'Poor kid…'

'Hopefully we can make a difference.' Anthony swallowed another mouthful of potato, then looked at her carefully. 'Can I ask you a personal question?'

'Of course.'

'Do you ever think about having kids again?'

And there it was. The question that haunted her. The question that her mother had asked her multiple times. The question that made her uncomfortable and desperate to avoid it. She wasn't sure she could answer him, so she did what she always did. Deflected.

'What about you? Do you see yourself having children one day?'

'I've always hoped to be a father. I wanted it to happen with Yael, but obviously that didn't work out. And I don't want to enter a relationship and have a child just to fulfil some destiny and heritage decreed by my birth and title. I'd want a child because I was in a serious, committed relationship with someone. A child born from true love and for no other reason.'

'So you can envisage yourself marrying again?' she asked, curious.

He shrugged. 'I don't know. Yael told me to find someone to be with. To not be alone. To find someone who makes my heart lift the way she did. But I'm not sure I'd ever be brave enough to put myself out there and risk having my heart broken again if I were to lose them.'

'It's difficult, isn't it?'

She understood his pain and reticence. Becoming a mother had been everything. To lose Marcus had ripped out her heart. Sometimes she yearned to have a baby to hold. To watch one grow. But could she do something that would terrify her?

'You and I are so different, and yet so similar in many ways. Maybe it's because I'm a dreamer and a romantic. I want a *guaranteed* happy-ever-after.'

'Life doesn't give guarantees, though,' said Anthony.

'No, it doesn't. So maybe we both need to just grasp true moments of happiness when we can? Not to expect a happy-ever-after, where we head into the sunset, knowing that everything will be perfect. Instead, we should grasp and keep hold of the small moments, and hope that by the time we're old and grey—if we're lucky enough to get old and grey—we have enough happy moments to make us smile each time we remember them?'

Anthony smiled. 'Sounds lonely, though.'

'We're not alone. We've found each other, after all these years, and we're doing something to help one another. I don't know about you, but that makes me smile. And no matter what happens...no matter which direction our lives take us in, even if they take us to opposite ends of the earth... I will always look back on our time together and be grateful for it.'

'To friendship?' He lifted a fork filled with potato and chilli.

'To friendship!' She touched her fork to his and felt a warmth inside her heart at having found herself a true friend. Someone who understood her fears. He didn't dismiss them, like her own mother sometimes did, telling her that she'd find someone

one day and everything would be okay. He just accepted them.

And that was all she needed, she told herself.

She hoped it was the truth. Because no matter how wonderful Anthony was, he could not offer her what she needed—and she couldn't give him what he needed, either.

When they'd finally eaten their fill, and could eat no more, Julia turned to look at the fountain. There were some kids playing in the water on the other side of it because it was such a nice, warm evening.

She turned back to look at Anthony's feet.

'What?' he asked.

'You ever gone paddling in a fountain?'

Anthony gave a half-laugh and looked behind him. 'Isn't that…er…illegal?'

'I don't see anyone arresting those kids.'

'I'm not sure we should.'

'Come on! Live a little! Break a rule and be happy.'

Julia began to reach down for her own shoes, slipping them off her feet and removing the little anklet socks that she'd got on underneath. Then she stood and stepped over the rim of the fountain and into the water, gasping at the coldness.

'It's fun! Come on!'

He looked at her and laughed. 'Okay, but if we get arrested I'm telling the judge that you drove me to it.'

'Fine.' She held out her hand once he'd slipped off his brogues and peeled off his dark socks.

He shook his head, almost as he couldn't believe he was going to do what she was encouraging him to do, and then took her fingers in his.

She felt a frisson of something tremble up her arm at his touch, the feel of his hand in hers bringing an awareness that went beyond mere friendship. The shiver was from the cold water, though. Surely?

'See? It's fun,' she said, trying to distract herself from the feeling of needing more.

'It's freezing—and there are pennies in here.'

'Not pennies. *Wishes.*' She laughed, suddenly nervous.

He was still holding her hand, still gazing into her eyes as with his free hand he pulled a coin from his pocket. A five pence piece. Small and silvery.

He passed it to her. 'Make a wish!'

Julia shook her head. 'It's your coin. You make the wish.'

'All right.'

'Close your eyes,' she said, watching as he stood still and slowly closed his eyes. Then with a flick of his finger the coin spun high into the air and came splashing down into the water between them. 'What did you wish for?'

Anthony smiled. 'That would be telling.'

Julia knew what she would have wished for as she gazed at his handsome, smiling face and her gaze dropped to his lips…

* * *

'Nurse, if you could change Mrs Mackie's dressing, please?'

'Yes, Mr Fitzpatrick.'

Mrs Mackie was an outlier patient who had been brought to the orthopaedic ward because there'd been no room for her elsewhere in the hospital at the time. She was an elderly woman, in her seventies, who had come into A&E after trying to break up a fight between two of her cats, using her stockinged foot. Her foot had been ripped to shreds by cat claws, and her thin, friable skin had developed an infection. They were treating it with larvae therapy, in which maggots would eat away at the dead skin and keep the wound clean.

'How is it feeling, Mrs Mackie?'

'A little sore, but I think better. These tiny pets aren't causing me any issues.'

'So no increased pain? That's good.'

Anthony watched as Julia cut away most of the bandaging and then, as she got closer to the biologics, slowed to make sure she didn't aggravate the wounds. The last layer was a piece of gauze soaked in sodium chloride, which she peeled off slowly, revealing the larvae bag, which she removed.

He bent over the patient's foot to examine it and smiled. 'Well, they've certainly done a very good job. You see how all the dead and infected tissue has been eaten away?'

Mrs Mackie nodded, intrigued.

'I think Nurse, that we can now move on to normal dressings—if you could get that done for me?'

Julia nodded to him and smiled. 'Yes, Mr Fitzpatrick.'

'I should imagine if you continue to heal without developing any further infection we can get you home soon. I'm going to arrange for the physios to come and give you some exercises you can do, and someone from Occupational Health to come and talk to you about how to manage at home.'

'Home? How soon?'

'Maybe in a couple of days? I just want to keep an eye on these wounds…make sure they start closing up properly on their own.'

'All right. Thank you.'

'You're welcome.'

'What will happen to them?' Mrs Mackie asked.

He had to admit he was a little confused by her question. 'What will happen to whom?'

'The maggots?'

'They'll be destroyed.'

'Seems such a shame when they did such a good job.'

He smiled and moved on to the next bed.

Patients never failed to surprise him.

'I have news!' Julia said as she swung open her front door.

'Hello to you, too,' Anthony said, as he leaned in to drop a kiss onto her cheek.

As excited as she was to share her news, she still felt a blush fill her cheeks with an enticing heat at his kiss. She wondered how it might feel to kiss him on the lips…

'I have news,' she said again.

'What is it?'

'Gramma May is doing so well they're talking of letting her home in a couple of days. Her speech is much better, and she's gained strength back in her affected arm.'

'That's fantastic!'

'I know! I told you she had nine lives.'

'I'm really happy for you.'

'Thanks. Now, are you ready for this?'

'As ready as I'll ever be.'

They were going to start work on the float for the parade. Her friend Paulie owned a large garage and they'd all agreed to work there.

'I think you'll get on well with Paulie,' she said.

'Have you known him long?'

'Quite a few years. He's the local mechanic and he fixed my tyre and collected my car that night when I got stranded near your place.'

'Sounds a good guy.'

'He is.'

'Who else is going to be there?'

'I think Janine. She was at university with me and now works in the critical care ward of St Agatha's Hospital in Surrey. Then there's Yvette, Paulie's wife. She's been sewing drapey curtains to hide the wheels all around the truck to make it look like it's floating.'

'What's the float going to be?'

'Castle in the sky. So we're going to be making clouds and a castle, with platforms for all our heroes and heroines to stand upon.'

'Great!'

'You're sure you're up for this? I'd hate to get any splinters in those surgical hands.'

'Splinter-schminter. I want to help. I'm *happy* to help.'

'Okay. Let's go!'

It wasn't far to the garage. About a twenty-minute drive. When they arrived everyone else was already there. Yvette and Janine were working out how to attach the drapes to the truck, whilst Paulie was sorting out wooden batons to construct the castle.

'Hi, guys. I've brought reinforcements. This is Anthony.'

The others stopped what they were doing to say hello, and there was a little bit of a chinwag for a while, and then they began working.

Julia was soon helping Anthony and Paulie to construct the base for the castle. 'A bit more over to the left, Anthony? About an inch?' she asked.

'Yep, that's it.'

Paulie had a power drill and connected two batons with a screw. 'Now the other end,' he said.

Essentially, they were constructing a rectangular base that would fit on the truck bed. They wanted to build two small rectangles to go on top of that, so the castle was tiered. With Paulie's tools, they made short work of it.

'Okay, we need to put this sheeting on the top of each layer. Ant, can you give me a hand carrying it over?'

Julia noticed that Paulie had started calling Anthony 'Ant'. He didn't seem to mind, and she had to admit she liked seeing Anthony fit in with her friends, getting to know them. She also liked watching his muscles flex as he carried things and hammered things. The look of concentration on his face…the easy way he fitted in with everyone.

'He's a good guy,' Janine said as they stood in the small kitchen to make tea for everyone.

'He is,' Julia agreed.

'Handsome.' Her friend raised an eyebrow.

'Yes.' She blushed. He *was* very handsome.

'What's he like?'

Julia frowned, not sure what she meant. 'How do you mean?'

'You know!' Janine grinned. 'In bed!'

'Wow.' Julia laughed nervously.

She'd stopped short of trying to imagine what he might be like in bed. She'd thought about kissing him passionately, and what that might feel like—of course she had. For their plan to work there might be an occasion when they needed to be seen sharing 'a moment', and she'd wondered where that might possibly lead. If his hands might wander a little bit.

But she'd always stopped short of thinking beyond that. The excitement of it thrilled her in a way that scared her. But she kept telling herself it was pointless—because that would never happen between them, even though she liked him very much. Their relationship was pretend.

But, as a hopeless romantic, of course she'd thought of what it might be like to be his girlfriend for real. Wouldn't anybody? And she'd seen sometimes that he looked at her in a certain way, so she could never be quite sure if he was attracted to her too, in some small way. But it would have to be a small way, because surely he wasn't really interested in her?

'We've…er…not gone that far yet,' she answered, being as honest as she could, considering the situation between them. 'We're taking it slowly.'

'Oh… I was hoping for a few juicy details!' Janine grinned. 'Being single myself, you know I like to live vicariously through others. What about you, Yvette?'

'I've been married for years—what do you think?'

Janine shrugged. 'I don't know. Does Paulie still drive you wild?'

Yvette laughed. 'He has some skills.'

'Yes! Tell me his best move.'

Julia laughed and picked up the tea tray to take it out to the two guys still working hard in the garage. She didn't need to hear about Paulie's 'best move' to thrill his wife in bed.

'Tea break.'

Paulie and Anthony had worked hard to create the basic structure, and now they were using the hammer gun to attach the second base onto the largest rectangular structure.

'Perfect,' Paulie said. 'No biscuits?'

'I can get some if you like?'

'No, it's fine. I'm watching my figure.' He winked, rubbing at his slight paunch. 'Yvette wants me beach-body-ready for when we hit Jamaica later in the year. You ever been there, Ant?'

'No, actually, I haven't.'

'You should go, mate. Amazing people…beautiful beaches. It's got this vibe, you know?'

Anthony smiled. 'I'll add it to my bucket list.'

'So! You two been going out long?'

'About a month?' Julia looked to Anthony to clarify.

'Something like that, yeah. It's hard to know exactly when it started, what with us working together.'

'And how is that? Dating and working together?'

'He hasn't got sick of me yet.' Julia laughed.

'Well, why would he?' Paulie asked, slurping at his mug of tea and slapping his lips together in appreciation. 'You've got a good one here, Ant, mate. You take care of her, all right?'

'I will.'

Julia looked at Anthony and smiled at him. Was this a moment to kiss him? Should she do that? She felt that a real couple would at this point.

But her hesitation made her miss the moment. Anthony just smiled at her and sipped his tea, unaware of the turmoil of her thoughts.

'When you find the right woman you just know, don't you?' Paulie continued. 'Look at me and Yvette. Everyone said we wouldn't work out, because we were so different, but look at us now. Married nearly ten years and happy as Larry.'

'Congratulations,' Anthony said.

'Cheers, mate. Well, I think we should call an end to this for the day. Next time we can make the remaining platform, stick it all together and then start painting—what do you say?'

'Sounds like a plan to me,' Anthony said.

'Yeah. Great,' Julia said. 'Though I'm not sure if Anthony will be able to make it to all these sessions.'

Anthony turned to her. 'I'll make it. I like spending my time with you.'

She blushed, not sure what to say.

But Paulie was. 'Aww…you two lovebirds. Makes me happy to see Julia smiling again.'

CHAPTER TEN

ANTHONY WAS ESCORTING MUSA, the young man who'd come over from Africa to have his legs operated on after suffering polio. He'd spent hours in Theatre with him, lengthening the tightened ligaments and getting rid of deformed muscle. Musa had also needed a total knee arthroplasty in his left leg—a knee replacement.

The surgery had gone very well indeed. But, as with most of his paediatric patients, Anthony liked to sit with them in Recovery and then escort them back to the ward. It was just a thing he did.

As he walked along the corridor with Musa, he spotted Julia at the reception desk.

'Nurse? Which bay for Musa?'

He saw Julia wipe at her eyes before turning round. 'Bay fourteen, please.'

Had she been crying? He felt his stomach lurch, not knowing why she was upset, but he knew he needed to get Musa settled first. Then he would come and see her.

Once he had Musa in his bay and comfortable,

and had promised to check on him in another hour or so, Anthony went to find Julia. He saw her go into the utility room, and glanced around to make sure no one was watching before he went in.

'Are you all right?' he asked.

She gave a short, embarrassed laugh. 'Yes! I'm fine!' she said, as she bent down to look for something on a shelf.

The shelf was filled with a variety of linens that were used to make up the beds. Sheets, blankets, pillowcases… There were also pyjamas and dressing gowns for those patients who didn't bring in their own, or those who arrived in A&E and were brought up to the ward not knowing that they would be kept in.

'You look upset,' he told her.

'It's fine. Honestly. You should go before people find us in here together.'

The tone of her voice told him something. That this was the thing that was bothering her.

'Has someone said something to you?'

She stopped. Straightened. Closed her eyes, then nodded.

'What's been said?'

'Another nurse said that she's noticed our interactions are different to anyone else's. That she can see that something's going on and that she expected better from a newly qualified nurse. She said that if I was sleeping with you, I ought to be ashamed.'

She began to cry. 'This is exactly what I was trying to avoid!'

He felt incredibly guilty, then. He'd not thought they would hurt anyone with their ruse, and he'd honestly tried to treat her like everyone else at work, but maybe he hadn't? Maybe it had been clear to anyone with eyes that Mr Ice's interactions with Nurse Morris were different. Softer. Kinder. Maybe his gaze lingered too long upon her? Maybe he smiled too much when he spoke to her? Maybe he called on her to assist him more than any of the other nurses? His preference to be with Julia had obviously created a bias and others had noticed. And rather than tell *him* about it, they had gone to the one with less power. The easier target.

And all because he'd wanted to get his mother off his back for a few weeks. He should have been better. A better Mr Ice.

He'd never wanted to hurt her professionally. It had never crossed his mind that he would.

Without thinking, he stepped towards her and pulled her into his arms. At first he felt her resistance, and he was about to let go, not wanting to make things worse, but then she relaxed against him and put her arms around him too, snuffling into his shirt. And even though she was upset, it felt really good to have her back in his arms. Pressed up against him. He was just holding her. Comforting her. It felt right. As if she was meant to be there. And it was his damn right to be able to do this for her.

Anger stirred within him at the unknown person who had upset her and the urge to go out there and defend her name washed over him briefly, before he let the anger go and just relaxed into the hug. He would stand there with her for hours if need be.

'Do you want me to talk to them? Put them straight?'

She shook her head.

'Who was it?'

'It doesn't matter.'

'You shouldn't be bullied.'

'It wasn't bullying. She said it like she was really disappointed in me, and it stung a bit. My reputation is very important to me.'

She didn't need to tell him that she'd hate anyone thinking she was just trying to land a doctor. That that was all she was here for. He knew she wanted to help people. She wanted to be respected. She'd come to this career later than others...

And then she seemed to realise what she was doing, and she let him go and stepped back, wiping her eyes. 'Better not. Anyone could come in.'

'Do you want me to leave?' He wanted to go on holding her. To comfort her.

'I want you to treat me like everyone else.' She looked him in the eye, her voice hard.

'I've been trying.'

'Try harder.'

And that was when he saw her strength. Her determination. And he knew then how she'd managed to get through those dark days when she'd lost Marcus. Because Julia was made of stern stuff. She had a steel core. A determination to make things right. Look at how eventually she'd turned her life around. Knowing that something needed to change. Taking on a new career path. Going to university as a mature student. Getting through her nursing education and passing all her modules with distinction. He could do nothing but admire her fortitude and bravery—if anything, she could only go up in his estimation.

'It's going to be hard to pretend that you're just anyone when you mean so much to me.'

She looked at him, then, with warmth and appreciation in her eyes. Her voice softened. 'You mean a lot to me, too.'

He was glad. That made him feel good. That it was reciprocated. 'I'd better go, then.'

'Yes…'

'I've just brought Musa down from Theatre.' It seemed best to change the subject.

'The boy from Africa?'

'Yes. His surgery went very well, but he won't have many visitors, so if all the staff could make an extra effort to look after him…make him feel that he's not alone?'

'Of course.'

He turned to go, his hand on the door handle,

but then he stopped. 'If anyone says anything else to you I want you to come to me and let me know. We're in this together, you and I. You shouldn't bear the brunt of any accusations.'

Julia nodded.

Satisfied, he left the room. Her words had made him feel sickened. That another nurse should say that to her... His eyes scanned the ward, looking at the other nurses he could see and wondering if it was one of them?

She would never tell him—he knew that—but he wished he knew.

Because right now he felt as if he would go to the ends of the earth to protect her.

Back at Paulie's garage, the construction of the castle had been completed and now everyone was wielding a paintbrush to decorate the float. Julia had a light blue paint, which she'd already managed to get on her hands and her clothes, and opposite her, at the far end of the truck, was Anthony. He had a white colour that he was using to paint the fake clouds that Paulie had carved out of thin MDF boards.

Today's accusation from Rosaria had stung.

Julia had been feeling so good beforehand. She'd just managed a difficult cannulation on a patient who'd kept pulling out her tubes and had earned a promise from her that she wouldn't do so again. She'd been tidying up and putting the rubbish into clinical waste when Rosaria, an older and more experienced nurse, who had worked on the ward for ten years or more now, had come up to her and said those words that had upset her quietly into her ear.

She'd thought Rosaria was a friend. She'd thought the senior and much-respected nurse respected *her* in turn. She'd said those words about her sleeping with Anthony as if she'd been giving her a warning, and when she'd protested that she wasn't sleeping with him, the older woman had simply rolled her eyes and said, *'Protest as much as you like, love. It's obvious there's something going on between you two. A man doesn't look at a woman like that unless something's going on.'*

Her protests had fallen on deaf ears, and the more she'd protested her innocence, the more Rosaria had looked disappointed in her for lying, and after that Julia hadn't known how to feel. She'd been so upset she'd had to take herself off to an empty room for a cry, hiccupping and gulping her way back to normal.

Wiping her eyes when she'd emerged from the room, she'd hoped no one would be able to tell that she'd been crying. And she thought she'd done okay until Anthony had seen her.

Of course he'd noticed. She'd tried to downplay it. She didn't want Rosaria to get into trouble. Julia hadn't been in her position long enough to feel that she could openly challenge a popular nurse with over a decade's worth of experience on this ward.

She gazed at Anthony now, across the other side of the float structure. He was smiling, listening to Paulie as he told him some story about a holiday he'd taken with his wife Yvette.

Anthony was really concentrating on his painting. He'd told Julia on the way over that he'd never painted a thing in his life and hoped he wouldn't do a bad job, and here he was anyway. Concentrating hard. Eyes focused. Carefully applying his brush strokes as if he were a master artist working on a portrait, or something. He'd begun to fit into her life so well. Her friends loved him. Her family loved him—especially for helping Gramma May. He'd tried to protect her at work, and she loved how thoughtful and kind he was, wanting to look out for her like that. But was this getting too complicated?

She'd not meant to start developing feelings for him, but if she'd been looking for a relationship to get into, he'd be just the kind of guy she'd go for. Forget that he was a duke. Forget that he was a surgeon. Those titles didn't matter. It was who he was as a person that she liked very much. Kind-hearted. Loving. Funny. Generous.

Loyal.

She realised, as they sat there painting, that she truly felt she would be able to trust him, and that was a big thing for her. She'd trusted Jake before she'd learned the truth about him already being married. And he hadn't been prepared to leave his marriage even though she'd been pregnant with his child. He'd made her feel that she didn't matter. That she and the baby weren't enough. Other guys she'd met through dating apps had been all shades of wrong, too, making her feel like something to be used. And yet she didn't feel like that when she was with Anthony.

What would it be like to date Anthony for real?

Perhaps all men seemed perfect until you got to know them better.

The thought of being with him, though, sent a shiver of excitement through her. She could do it, couldn't she? She could pretend that it was real and experience it through the safety net of their pretence to their families. The fact was that this wouldn't last. It was only for a few weeks more. His mother would be flying to Adelaide soon. Perhaps if she was more physical? A touch? A kiss? Not just those pecks on the cheeks they'd been doing, but actually going in for a real kiss? On those delicious-looking lips of his? Nothing too prolonged. No tongues— nothing like that to begin with. Not unless he responded, of course, and they both got carried away in the moment...

He would be shocked, no doubt, but they had already told one another that they would kiss each other if the situation required it. They just hadn't done it yet. How would she be able to engineer the occasion? Or should it just come naturally?

Julia licked her own lips in anticipation of the idea of kissing Anthony and looked away. Her paintbrush had dropped away from the wood and more paint had dripped onto her trousers. She could imagine it. Picture it. The press of his lips. Would he sigh with pleasure? Would she?

'You're making a right mess there,' Yvette said, laughing. 'The paint's meant to go on the wood—not you.'

'Sorry!' Julia blushed. 'I was daydreaming.'

'Yeah…and I think I know what about.' Yvette winked at her and then looked knowingly at Anthony, before laughing again and leaning in quietly. 'It's okay. I remember that first flush of love, when he can do no wrong. I used to daydream about Paulie like that.'

'You don't daydream about him still?'

'Oh, yeah! But now my fantasies revolve around whether he'll get that kitchen tap fixed, or whether he can push the vacuum around whilst I read my book.'

Julia laughed. 'You love him still!'

'Yeah, he's not bad.'

'What made you fall in love with Paulie? What was it about him?'

'He could make me laugh. And he was very good with his hands!' She wiggled her eyebrows suggestively and laughed at herself. 'Most of all it was because he made me feel safe. Made me feel like I could just be me and he'd adore me for it. I didn't have to put on a mask to be with him. He just loved me...warts and all.'

Julia smiled. That sounded exactly like the type of relationship she would love to have. And she could have it. A ruse within another ruse. For a measly few pretend weeks and then it would be gone.

Who could it hurt?

What if the experiences they had together made them see that there could be something for them after this? A relationship? That they worked well together and it all made sense?

Anthony wasn't hiding anything about who he was with her. She knew his past and he knew hers. They both knew how the other one had been hurt, and knew they didn't want to feel that pain again. They were each other's safety net, weren't they? And wasn't that what Yvette had said about Paulie? That he made her feel safe?

'Anthony?'

'Yes?' He stopped painting to look at her, warmth and kindness in his eyes.

'After this, maybe we should go for a walk along the river. It's such a nice night... I think it will be great.'

He nodded. 'Sure!'

'You guys could go now, to be honest with you,'

said Paulie. 'There's not much more we can do tonight, before letting all of this dry.'

'I'll just finish this last baton, then,' Anthony said.

It was lovely and cool down by the river. There were people out on the water—some kayaking, one or two paddle boarding. Couples and families were sitting on the concrete steps just watching the world go by.

Anthony couldn't ever remember walking by a river like this. He'd been by lakes, salmon fishing. He'd crossed oceans on cruise liners. But this river—the River Tamblin, which was near Paulie's garage—he'd never walked beside. He'd not even known it existed. But apparently it meandered along the edge of the town and even had areas for paddling.

'We should do that,' Julia said.

'What?'

'Go paddling.'

He didn't understand. 'Why?'

'Because it's nice. Because it's fun. Like at the fountain.'

He had fond memories of that. Yes, it had been fun to paddle in the water—but it had been more fun to hold her hand and listen to her laugh and splash each other.

'Have you got a thing for messing about in water?' he asked, and smiled to show he was joking.

'I find it calming after a long day. Come on!'

'It's not clean…'

'You think the fountain was clean?'

He shrugged.

'Take off your shoes and socks. Roll up those jeans. It's soothing. Come *on*!'

Anthony marvelled at her. Sometimes it was as if she had the innocence of a young child. She loved puddles, she'd once told him. She could remember as a child walking up the street to her school in bright red wellington boots, holding her mother's hand whilst she splashed in the puddles that had gathered near the kerbs and gutters.

She'd splashed around in that water fountain the other day, and when she'd made him close his eyes to make a wish, her face turned up towards his, he'd thought how easy it would be to kiss her. Only he hadn't. Because he was a gentleman, and he would never do anything like that without her consent. And besides, they were only pretending to be in a relationship. They weren't actually in one.

And now she wanted to splash around at the river's edge… Why not?

So he bent down once again, removed his shoes and socks, and walked out into the water with her, holding her hand to keep her steady. He didn't want her to slip or fall, after all. This was a safety issue, he told himself.

He could feel mud beneath his toes, squelching through the gaps. Cold and soft. And although the sensation was incredibly weird to begin with, after a while he actually began to like it.

'You see?' she said.

'How often do you do this?' he asked. 'Mess about in water?'

'As often as I can. It makes me feel… I don't know…kind of free. Kind of empty of all my woes and worries for a little while.'

He nodded. 'It's relaxing for you?'

'Yes. You can't imagine how many times I did this when I was studying to be a nurse. I'd take exams and then, instead of waiting at home, worrying about the results and whether I'd passed, I would find somewhere to paddle. You can forget about being an adult for a while. It's good for you.'

'Why don't you just go swimming at a leisure centre?'

She stopped to look at him. 'Because that would be too busy. Too loud and echoey. Out here, I can be in nature. Birds singing. Blue skies…'

'Muddy water?'

Julia laughed and turned back to look at him. Then she looked down at their hands, still holding one another. 'Have you thought about us kissing?' she asked suddenly, looking serious.

He hoped his cheeks didn't colour and betray him. Because of course he had! He'd thought about kissing her for real every single time he'd leaned in and dropped a kiss on her cheek. He'd dreamed about kissing her every time she'd looked at him and smiled. There was something in the way that she looked at him… It went straight to his heart.

But surely she didn't mean that? 'You mean to help the illusion we're creating with our families?' he asked.

She shrugged. 'Sure.'

'We do kiss. We've done it in front of them.'

'Pecks on the cheek. Polite kisses. I mean…' She seemed to swallow. 'Proper kisses.'

His gaze dropped to her mouth. 'On the lips?'

'Where else?'

'How…how do you mean?' He wasn't sure what to say. What to admit to. What was she actually asking him, here?

'Well, if this ruse is going to work properly, I think that, on occasion, we may have to kiss each other on the lips the way a proper couple would.'

'Right…'

'And we don't want that to be awkward, do we? We want it to look…natural.'

'Comfortable?'

'Yes.'

Her gaze had dropped to his lips. Ever so briefly. Then she met his gaze again and her cheeks were flushed with a rosy glow.

'What do you propose?' he asked.

She laughed and looked away, her gaze taking in the couples, the families, a dog splashing into the water, chasing after a ball that had been thrown for it to retrieve.

'That maybe…maybe we ought to practise? So that it looks natural for us.'

He realised her tone was trying to make her suggestion sound as reasonable and as logical as possible.

'We don't want to kiss and look awkward…or clash teeth or anything…'

He thought about what she was suggesting.

Practice-kissing.

She did have a point. They'd need to look as if they'd kissed before. Many times! And if they practised, then that would be true, right?

'All right. Seems sensible.'

He tried to sound as if it was simply a sensible idea. A logical idea. When in reality his heart was pounding as if he'd run a marathon. Was she truly just being sensible about this? Or did she really want to kiss him? A part of him wished for the latter—even though that, in itself, would be terrifying.

She looked at him. 'Yeah? Okay… So, maybe we should do that?'

He looked around them. 'Here?'

'No. Not here. Not with an audience like this!' She laughed.

'Somewhere private?'

Julia nodded.

'Back in the car?'

His heart was thudding. He was imagining himself in such a small, confined space with Julia. Kissing her.

'Sounds as good a place as any.'

'Okay.'

'Okay…'

They stood there in the water for a little longer, not saying anything.

'When do you want to…?' he asked.

'Let's go and do it now,' she said, blushing madly.

He nodded. 'No time like the present,' he agreed, trying to sound reasonable.

CHAPTER ELEVEN

THEY WALKED IN SILENCE back towards the car, the air between them heavy with intent and expectation.

Julia had not expected him to agree to her suggestion so easily. Or so quickly. Had she expected him to laugh it off? Say it wasn't necessary? Or maybe even say that he would feel weird doing so? But perhaps he was keen to kiss her too? No, most likely he wanted their fake relationship to look real. He'd already told her he wasn't ready to be in another relationship. It was the whole reason they were together in the first place.

Would she be the first woman to kiss him seriously, since Yael? Surely not? Surely a guy like Anthony would have had many opportunities?

But he hadn't laughed it off. He'd seemed keen, too. Perhaps he'd even thought of this issue himself, but hadn't known how to raise the subject? Maybe he was glad that she had done so instead?

They were here. They'd arrived at the car park and she found herself going round to the passenger side of the car as Anthony went to the driver's side and unlocked the doors. She gave him one lingering glance before she got in, encouraged to see that he seemed as nervous as she was.

Julia slid into her seat and closed the door with a sense of finality. She rubbed her hands along her thighs, in case they were damp—which they were not.

She sucked in a breath and gave a small laugh. 'How do you want to do this?'

'Well, why don't you tell me how you would like this to proceed? Maybe establish a few ground rules? A safe word?'

She nodded. 'Good. Yes. Okay. Maybe our safe word ought to be something one of us would say a lot…so maybe something from work?'

He nodded. 'So it would sound like we were talking about a case? What word would be good? But also sound like a way to tell the other person to stop?'

Julia thought. 'How about *patient*?'

Anthony smiled and nodded. 'Perfect.'

'Okay. Safe word chosen. Ground rules…'

'I never thought I would ever have to have ground rules for kissing,' he said.

'No, nor me. But in this situation it might make us both feel a little better about doing it,' she said, as if kissing Anthony was going to be some sort of chore. She strongly suspected that it would not be, but you never could tell. Not until you did it. 'I honestly don't know where to start.'

'Well, what about my hands? Where would you be happy with me placing them?'

She could feel her cheeks colour as she imagined all the places he *could* put them. But they had to be sensible here, and remember the impression they would give others.

'I guess we have to think about what other people would expect to see. Maybe around my waist?'

He nodded. 'I could do that. What about…' he turned in his seat to look at her properly '…if I cupped your face? Like so?'

Her lips parted and her breathing increased as his hands came up to cup her jawline. Softly. Reverently. His wonderful touch was, oh, so gentle.

'Would this be all right?' he asked, looking deeply into her eyes.

It meant she was staring deeply into his too. Not trusting herself to speak right then, all she could do was nod.

'Could my fingers go into your hair? Push back a strand, like this?'

She felt his fingers deftly delve into the hair at the nape of her neck. Felt a finger from his other hand tidy away a strand behind her left ear before he cupped her face again. She could imagine his fingers trailing elsewhere. Touching. Feeling. Exploring.

She gulped. 'That…that would be fine,' she managed, her voice croaky. His eyes were *so blue*. Like small oceans with hidden depths of beauty if only she cared to dive deeper.

'And when I kiss you…'

'Yes?'

'Closed mouth or…more?'

Had his voice grown hoarse too? Her gaze dropped to his lips. Parted, like hers. How would she like him to kiss her? Softly, yes. Tenderly. What would he taste like? He was asking her permission to be able to taste her, too, though she couldn't imagine they'd be doing any full-on snogging in front of his mother…

'Either's fine.'

It was all she could think of to say. She was imagining it. Imagining his tongue delving deep into her mouth to find hers and entwining with it. She wanted it all! Wanted to try all of his kisses and pretend they were real. But she had to pretend that this was pretend! To maintain the pretence!

I'm going to die.

'Okay…' he breathed. 'I guess those are the rules.'

She nodded, though her head was still held within his gentle grasp.

'I guess all that's left to do, then, is…kiss.'

'I guess so.'

Her heart was pounding out of her chest. Thudding and thumping like a wild animal madly trying to escape her ribcage. Her face felt hot, her skin tingling. She tried to slow her heartbeat, to remain in control. To act as if this was nothing. Because she couldn't let him know how badly she wanted this to be real.

He leaned in. Slowly. She could feel his breaths—rapid, like her own—and she wondered if he was craving the kiss as much as she was.

'Wait!' she said suddenly.

'What is it?'

'We haven't come up with your rules.'

'Oh. Right.'

She smiled shyly. 'Where can I put *my* hands? Here?' She leaned in and gently placed her hands upon his chest. She could feel his heart pounding beneath her fingertips.

He nodded.

'Okay.'

'Okay. You ready?'

'Yes. Are you?'

'Yes.'

'Okay…'

Anthony leaned in again. Slowly. Inching forward. Making sure that she still wanted this.

She wanted nothing more. She'd been craving his kiss for so long now she couldn't quite believe that it was about to happen. At long last.

She closed her eyes as his lips met hers and her world imploded. The kiss was sensuous, hot, and it thrilled her every sense and nerve and heartbeat. His tongue met hers in a warm embrace and time grew still as if only they existed and only they moved…as if they were an anomaly compared to the rest of the universe. Julia felt dizzy, as if she needed to come up for air, but strangely *he* was her air, and her oxygen, and she felt that she could stay kissing him for ever.

It felt perfect. It felt right. It felt…hot! Tantalising…erotic. Her body came alive at his touch and she felt the desire to pull open his shirt, rip away those buttons, to find her hands touching his skin, his flesh, feeling the heat of him, the strength of him, those muscles… She wanted to trail her fingers down his chest, across his abs, lower…lower… and then…

And then the kiss was over, much too soon, and he pulled back slightly to look at her with glazed eyes.

'Was that all right?' he whispered softly.

All right?

Was that *all right*?

It had been more than all right! She was out of breath, stunned by everything she had felt and amazed she could even make her brain work enough to form a coherent response. It wasn't enough. She needed more. To see that it wasn't just a fluke, but that it would feel like that with him every time!

'Yes. Should we…do it again? Just to…you know…feel *really* comfortable?'

A small smile curved the corners of his beautiful, delicious mouth. 'One more time, then. For good luck.'

And he kissed her again.

* * *

Anthony totally forgot that this was just *practising*. That this was just a *rehearsal* in case they had to do the real thing in front of people one day in the next few weeks. To look *authentic*.

Kissing Julia made him forget the world. Made everything else simply melt away at the feel of her lips upon his. She was warm, and she tasted of mint, and of orange from the juice that she'd had at Paulie's. His hands were in her hair and, by God, he had to fight the urge to let them wander.

He was sorely tempted, but she'd not agreed to his hands going anywhere apart from where they were and on her waist, and if he let them explore… let them touch, feel, stroke…then she would stop the kiss. She would say *patient*, their safe word, and he did not want to break her trust. She'd already explained to him how she felt she couldn't trust men, not after what Marcus's father had done to her, and she was trusting him to stick to their ground rules. So he would.

But…

He'd not kissed a woman like this for a very long time, and his senses were going into overload. His body was afire with need and desire after being starved of affection and touch for so long. His head felt scrambled and stunned.

When they broke apart she gazed at him uncertainly, and then leaned back into her own seat, her fingers touching her lips, before she smiled at him.

She looked so beautiful in that moment—so shy, so innocent... Even though that kiss they'd just shared had been nothing like innocent.

He cleared his throat. 'Well, I think we've got that covered, don't you?'

Julia nodded. 'I thought it was very convincing.' She gave a strange sated smile.

'Me too.'

What were they supposed to do now? Act as if nothing had happened?

'Shall I take you home?' he asked.

She glanced at her watch. 'It is starting to get late...and we have work tomorrow.'

He started the engine as he tried to cool down. It felt weird that he wanted more. He'd not felt this way in a long time, and he'd never imagined he would find a passion for someone like this ever again. The idea that he might have a fulfilling life after Yael had seemed impossible. And yet here he was. Considering it.

But no. This is all just an illusion. She didn't mean any of what we just did. It was just acting. And I'd do well to remember that.

CHAPTER TWELVE

ROSARIA LOOKED UP at Julia as she came onto the ward the next morning. She'd been on a night shift, and would be doing the handover for the day shift.

'Morning, Rosaria!' said Julia. 'How was last night?'

'Well, I hesitate to use the Q word, but it actually was.'

Quiet. She meant quiet. They tried not to use that word to describe a shift, because the second they did, usually all hell would break loose.

'Great. See you in a few minutes.'

'Yes, you will.'

Julia disappeared into the staff room. She hung up her things in her locker, and then took her water bottle and placed it in the fridge before going to make herself a quick cup of tea.

Other staff arrived in dribs and drabs.

'Hey, Jo.'

'Debs! How are you?'

'Living the dream.'

'And experiencing a nightmare?'

Julia smiled at the familiar start-of-shift banter as she took one of the handover sheets, grabbed a pen from her top pocket and waited for Rosaria to come in and begin.

The older nurse came in and stood at the front of the room, waiting for the hustle and bustle to die down, and then she began.

As she'd said, it seemed the orthopaedic ward had had a quiet night. Most of the patients had slept soundly, with only bed three needing an extra dose of painkillers as he wasn't coping with his pain levels. Musa, the young man who'd had polio, was recovering well and had begun to eat again after feeling sick for a few days after the anaesthetic. And they'd had a new patient arrive from A&E, who had fallen down the stairs in the middle of the night and fractured his back as well as his arm. He would be going down for surgery this morning, to be put back together again.

There were no outstanding jobs to carry over onto the day shift so they had a fresh start, when all they had to do was get everyone washed and dressed, if they could be, then fed, and then do the drugs round, before their new patient got called for surgery.

'That's it! Best of luck!' Rosaria said, and they all began to file out and take over from the night shift staff. 'Julia? Could I have a quick word?'

Julia started, and then nodded.

Oh, no. I hope she's not going to say something else about me and Anthony.

Because if she did, her blushes from the knowledge that she'd now kissed Anthony passionately would probably overwhelm her.

Julia waited for the room to empty, then turned to the older nurse. 'Everything all right?'

'No, it's not.' Rosaria gave a sigh. 'I need to make an apology to you.'

'Oh, there's no need to do that!'

Because you were right.

'There is. I was out of line the other day, suggesting that there was something going on with you and a senior colleague on the ward without direct evidence, and I said some unkind and unfair things. I was particularly tired and stressed that day, and I took out my frustrations about things going on in my life on you, which I know is no excuse. So, I apologise.'

Julia was shocked. She'd not expected Rosaria to apologise at all. And honestly there *was* something going on between her and Anthony—just not what Rosaria thought. Julia felt guilty that she had to hide it from her colleague, but it was important for her to be seen as a professional—especially since she was only just starting out as a nurse and this job was very important to her.

She wanted to be like those nurses who had helped her after Marcus had passed. She wanted to provide the warmth that she'd received then. And if she helped just one person walk away from this hospital feeling that they were important, and not just another patient, then she would have achieved that. She was here for her patients. Not for anything else.

If something were to develop between her and Anthony…something real…then she would tell her colleagues. But only if it developed into something serious, like an engagement or a marriage. And she really didn't think that would happen. Anthony had made no suggestion that their kissing had changed anything for him. All they'd been doing was practising. Even if, for her, the kissing had been out of this world.

'I appreciate that, Rosaria, thank you,' she said quietly.

'So, we're good?'

She nodded. 'We're good.'

But she still felt guilty. As if she'd somehow made Rosaria apologise for nothing.

Julia was on the drugs round that morning. She donned a tabard that said *Do Not Disturb. Drug Round in Progress* on the back, and began taking the drugs cabinet from bed to bed, issuing medication to patients and marking the drugs issued on the patient's records. It was very important not to be disturbed whilst performing this task. It was so easy to make a mistake, to be distracted, and also, walking around with a cabinet filled with medication was a hazard. A risk. Medication was counted and had to be accounted for, and it was a job that each nurse took seriously.

As she went from patient to patient, saying good morning, asking them how they'd slept, issuing prescriptions, she noticed Anthony and his horde of junior doctors arrive. Instantly she felt her heartbeat escalate. How could she not? Those kisses of his had burned into her lips and her memory, and she'd gone to sleep that night dreaming of him.

'Morning, Nurse!' said her next patient, Thomasina Young, who was on the ward with a broken pelvis and neck of femur after a cliff fall.

'Morning, Thomasina. Sleep well?'

'Not really.'

'Oh, I'm sorry to hear that? Could you just not sleep? Or were you in discomfort?'

'Flashbacks to the fall. Every time I closed my eyes I kept experiencing it.'

Julia gave a sympathetic smile to her patient. She understood that. She'd experienced the same thing in the first few months after Marcus's passing. If she'd got to sleep, then she would suddenly wake with a start, heart pounding, fearing something was wrong. She would go rushing to his room, only to find it empty, all silent, and each time, it would break her heart. She'd been too late. Why hadn't she woken with a start the night he'd died?

Because I was exhausted. I hadn't slept properly for weeks.

She would stand in the doorway of his room and

remember that moment. The moment she'd entered his room that fateful morning and seen him lying peacefully in his cot. The realisation as she'd stared at his face and known that something had gone terribly wrong.

'Maybe I could ask the nurse in charge if you could have a sleeping tablet tonight? It's very important for you to get some decent rest after an injury like this.'

'They already offered me one, but I refused.'

'Why?'

'I think it's important for me to understand where I went wrong. If I keep reliving it, maybe one time I'll see my mistake.'

'You shouldn't let yourself be tormented like that.'

'Maybe, but it wasn't just me that got hurt. My fall hurt my friend. She got sent to another hospital and I'm responsible for that.'

'It sounds like you feel guilty.'

'I am.'

'But it was an accident. Accidents happen. You can't foresee everything that is going to happen.'

It was something she'd struggled with in the early days. Blaming herself. And though she'd hated it every terror-stricken time when she'd rushed to her son's room to check on him, she also, weirdly, hadn't minded it. Because in those few precious moments between her waking and arriving at her son's bedroom door in her mind there had been the possibility that he was still alive. That he was still with her.

Eventually, her doctor had prescribed sleeping tablets, which she'd begun to take, knowing she couldn't carry on the way she had been. Everyone had begun commenting on her appearance. How haggard she looked. The size of the bags and dark circles beneath her eyes. The sleeping tablets had helped get her back into a healthy sleeping pattern, but she'd still felt guilty every time she'd woken up without him.

'I'm sure your friend doesn't blame you,' she said now.

'She doesn't. I've talked to her on the phone. But that doesn't stop me from feeling guilty.'

'It'll pass. With time, it'll pass.' She didn't want to tell Thomasina that actually the guilt would remain…it would just get easier to carry.

That didn't sound half as good.

But it was the truth.

She would always feel that way about Marcus. If only she hadn't slept through… If only she'd gone and checked on him. Maybe he would still be here today and her life would be totally different. She wouldn't have become a nurse. She would never have met Anthony again.

A warm feeling spread through her at the thought of him, and she completed her drugs round in a very good mood indeed.

When she was done, she felt her mobile phone

vibrate in her uniform pocket, and checked it to see an invitation from Zoey, Anthony's sister.

It's my birthday tomorrow and I'm inviting the family. Do say you'll come! Seven p.m., Clareleas House. Zoey x

Of course. By dating Anthony, she was now considered *family*. She and Zoey had not yet made it out for that coffee they'd promised each other, but a birthday invitation was just as good, and she'd not seen any of his family since the ball. She knew she would need to talk to Anthony about it first, though, and if she was going she needed to know what kind of present to buy.

At lunchtime, she noticed Anthony in the cafeteria, eating his lunch. She wanted to go over to him, to talk about Zoey's invitation, but two tables away from Anthony, sat a group of nurses, and she didn't want to provoke more rumours. So she grabbed her own lunch and sat on the opposite side of the room and texted him.

She watched as he reached for his phone and pulled it from his pocket, and then she saw the delightful way his face brightened when he saw the text was from her.

It made her smile. He was unobserved. He had no way of knowing that she was watching him from afar.

Pretty soon, his answer arrived.

Sounds great. I'll pick you up at six-thirty. Smart casual will be fine. I'll buy her favourite perfume. A x

Julia loved it that he'd added a kiss after his initial. And the way he'd smiled at seeing her name on his phone. After the kissing, she felt that something had most definitely changed in her feelings for him, and she hoped that he'd felt the genuine change in her affections too.

It felt nice...what they had going on. Surprising. Unexpected. When he'd first suggested this ruse, to get their respective families off their backs, she'd never expected that her feelings might change. That she might come to hope for more. That she might want their feelings to become real. Because she'd never expected to trust a man ever again. She'd never expected to feel safe with a man who would not disrespect her in any way. And even though she'd hoped that in the future she wouldn't be alone, she'd not expected to feel so strongly for someone yet.

That it had happened with Anthony was truly lovely. Because she felt as if he'd been with her since the start of her story, all those years ago—when she was a waitress, and pregnant, and not only full of baby, but full of hope that she would forge a bright future for herself and her son. Her last decade had been spent in a grey fog, but since meeting Anthony again that fog had drifted away and she felt that her life was sunny again.

All because of how being with him made her feel.

From her table, she watched him get up and return his tray. He stopped briefly to converse with another surgeon. She thought he was from neuro, maybe. Anthony laughed, and the way his smile brightened his face made her smile, too, as the two men shook hands and parted ways.

Julia's gaze went to Rosaria, and she blushed when she realised Rosaria was watching her.

Clareleas House was a large new-build house constructed to look as if it had been built in the Georgian era. Brick-built, with symmetrical sash windows and a side gabled roof, it sat at the end of a long driveway bordered by dwarf willow trees.

Zoey and her husband Michael were there to greet Julia and Anthony as they arrived at the front door.

'Julia! How lovely to see you again! I adore that dress—whose is it?' Zoey asked, as if Julia was wearing some designer outfit.

She blushed. 'Oh, no one special. Off the rack.'

'Well, you look stunning in it—doesn't she Anthony?'

He had to admit that she did. But lately he'd begun to believe that Julia could wear a potato sack and still look amazing.

'Yes, she looks beautiful,' he agreed, leaning in casually to drape an arm around Julia's waist.

'Don't worry, brother dear, you look handsome,

too,' Zoey said, dropping a kiss onto his cheek. She turned then and grabbed her husband's hand. 'Julia? This is Michael, my hubby. He couldn't come to Mother's ball. He had a situation at work that needed his attention.'

'Pleased to meet you, Michael.' Julia shook his hand.

'You too. Always happy to meet another victim willing to get involved with the Fitzpatrick family.' He laughed.

Anthony laughed, too. 'I think that says more about you than it does about us.'

'Oh, I don't know, old boy. Come on in! Everyone else has already arrived and your mother is making her way through my wine collection. We need to get some food into her sharpish.'

Ah, he thought. *One of those evenings.*

When his mother's desire for grandchildren became overwhelming, because unhappily none of her children had yet produced heirs, she got a little tipsy as she turned to wine to make her feel better. His mother was no serious drinker, by a long shot, but every now and again she'd get maudlin about the fact that she had no grandchildren to spoil. And it seemed that today was going to be one of those days when she did.

'Let's hope Zoey hasn't sat you next to my mother at the table,' he whispered into Julia's ear, unwittingly inhaling her floral perfume and apple-scented shampoo.

He was thrown by the sensory overload, and the desire it prompted within him not to head to the dining room, but to a bedroom instead. Where he could explore all her other scents.

He honestly didn't know what was happening to him. Since meeting Julia again, his world had turned on its axis. Tilting wildly. Throwing all his expectations of what his life was going to be like into the air. And since the kissing practice he'd begun to feel a hunger for her that consumed him daily.

He was amazed he could feel this way. After Yael, he'd never thought he could have such strong feelings for another woman. But his connection to Julia was unlike anything he'd ever had before. Different from Yael. Different from anyone. He burned to be with her. He looked for her at the hospital. Just getting glimpses of her as she went about her work was enough and could make him smile. And the instances in which they could talk to one another, unobserved, brightened his day considerably. And when he couldn't see her or be with her he thought about her constantly.

These feelings, these desires, had come so fast, so intensely, that they worried him. What did it all mean? This wasn't a permanent thing. It was only for a few weeks. His mother flew to Adelaide soon, and would be gone for two months. As soon as she got on that aeroplane this illusion that he and Julia had created could stop.

And what would that feel like?

To return to normal?

Did he even *want* normal?

In the dining room, they greeted everyone. His mother, who dropped kisses on their cheeks, Zoey's friend Simon and his wife Harriet, Xavier and his fiancée Anna-Louise. And his mother had brought her friend Francesca, who was Zoey's godmother.

He could feel everyone's eyes on them as they moved around the room and he introduced Julia to them all. He kept a tight grip on her waist, taking reassurance from having her at his side. Normally at these events he would turn up alone and endure comments from everyone about how he needed to find someone and to settle down. How wonderful being part of a couple was. How no Duke of Weston had ever remained single and that he had a duty to provide an heir.

He would have loved to have a child with Yael, but they hadn't even got close to that goal. They'd had fun practising, though... In the early days, when they'd not known anything malignant was growing within her, they had been happy, carefree, fun. The hopes and possibilities for the future had seemed bright and available to them. As if the whole world could be theirs if they just reached for it.

And then cancer had reared its ugly head. Non-small cell lung cancer. Filling her lungs with fluid, metastasising to her brain and her bones and her liver. Into her lymph nodes. She'd fought so bravely, and for so long, holding on to hope each time she was given chemotherapy or immunotherapy or a new clinical trial when all the other possibilities had run out.

Yael would have made an excellent mother.

And now he was here, with Julia, his body craving her, his mind awash with her.

They'd barely sat down before the questions began.

'So how long have you two been together now?' his mother asked.

'Only a few weeks,' he said, hoping that such a short amount of time would be regarded by everyone else as not long enough to start asking them the heavy-hitting questions, like *Have you thought about getting engaged?* or *How many kids do you see yourself having?*

'Tick-tock, Anthony, darling. Tick-tock!' His mother laughed and sipped at her wine.

'Maybe you should make that your last glass, Mother, and move on to something more suitable. Say, black coffee?'

'Nonsense, darling! The night is yet young!'

Zoey made a motion to her staff to indicate that they ought to serve the first course and their plates arrived perfectly in time with each other. Smoked salmon with Greenland prawns, on a bed of salad with aioli sauce.

'This looks lovely, Zoey,' Julia said.

'Thank you. They're all my favourite dishes tonight, so I hope you like seafood?'

'I do. It's a favourite of mine, too.'

Zoey smiled. 'Tuck in, everyone.'

The first course went pleasantly enough. Anthony had Julia opposite him, his mother on one side and Zoey on the other. The three most important women in his life all around him. It would have been nice, if he hadn't felt so on edge.

'I know it's early days, Julia, and obviously you're a young woman with your career ahead of you, but do you ever think about the future?'

'Mother...' he warned.

'I'm just asking a simple question, darling.'

'Of course I do,' Julia answered diplomatically. 'I often wonder what it will hold.'

'Have you ever foreseen children as part of that future?' his mother persisted, determined in her line of questioning.

Julia blushed and sipped at her water, dabbing at her mouth with her napkin.

Of course his mother did not know about baby Marcus. That a child had already been a part of her life.

'Yes. I would very much like to have children in my future,' she answered, smiling.

Was she saying that because she was playing her part? Proving to his mother that he was in a relationship that might lead him the way his mother so desperately wanted? Or did she actually mean it?

Losing Marcus would have knocked her sideways. He couldn't imagine how it had affected her. After losing Yael, he'd felt he couldn't function without her in those early days. He'd wished he could have her back. Was Julia brave enough to go through all that uncertainty and fear if she had another child? She was indeed the bravest woman he knew, if that was the case.

Or maybe she didn't really want kids. He couldn't imagine being brave enough to take that on again. The fear would be unimaginable. And if she didn't want any more kids, could he still imagine a future with her? He'd figured he'd have them one day... just not on his mother's timeline, that was all.

'Excellent!' His mother took another sip of wine. 'Hopefully you can persuade my son to feel the same way at some point. He seems quite reluctant on that front.'

Julia glanced at him, and there was a warm, loving smile on her face as she reached for his hand upon the table, for everyone to see, and said, 'I respect Anthony enough to know he'll make up his own mind on what he wants and when he wants it. Especially after all he's been through. I don't believe in forcing anyone to do anything they're not ready for.'

He smiled back at her. No one had ever stood up to his mother like that before. They'd all been too polite to say anything that might upset the Dowager Duchess, who was a true force of nature.

Even his mother looked surprised. 'I know he's been through a lot, but he needs to move on. He can't stay single for the rest of his life—and it has been *ten years*,' she said, as if time somehow played a part in his decision.

Julia smiled. 'Grief has no timetable,' she said. 'Having children, getting married…these are all huge life changes. They don't always go smoothly, and your life is changed irreparably. Especially having children. They become your everything. They change who you are. Your outlook on life. They take up all of your time…your thoughts.'

'I know that, Julia!' his mother responded rather sharply. Too sharply. 'I have a son and daughter right here. And, forgive me, but you've never been a mother, so I'm not sure you have the right to sit there and tell me what sacrifices you have to make as a parent.'

Anthony felt Julia's grip on his hand tighten. He was going to speak, to try and smooth things over, but Julia spoke first.

'But that's where you're wrong, Your Grace. I am a mother. I am mother to a beautiful little boy called Marcus, who passed away ten years ago. I know about motherly sacrifice and worry. I know about how a child takes up your every consuming thought. He may no longer be here, but I am still Marcus's mother.'

Julia got up from the table and rushed away. All the other guests looked on, shocked, then turned to look at him, as if to confirm whether he knew about Marcus or not.

Anthony stood, dabbed at his mouth and stared down at his mother. 'You really need to think before you speak sometimes, Mother.'

As he stood, so did Zoey laying a hand upon his arm. 'I'll help you find her.'

'No. You stay here. Look after your guests. I'm sorry if we've spoilt your birthday.'

'You haven't.' She dropped a kiss upon his cheek and gave him a sympathetic smile.

Anthony left the dining room, trying to decide which way Julia might have gone.

A member of staff was just closing the front doors.

'Can I help you, sir?'

'Yes, I'm looking for Julia. The young lady I arrived with.'

'She's gone out to the rose garden, sir.'

'Thank you.'

The rose garden was beautiful, with a gentle scent in the air from the smorgasbord of blooms. Soft pinks, blood-reds, butter-yellows and creamy whites. In the centre of the garden was a circular wooden bench, enveloping the trunk of a large tree, and it was there that Julia sat, cursing softly at herself for allowing Anthony's mother to wind her up so badly.

Yes, the older woman had been drinking, and

Julia should have taken her words with a pinch of salt, but the woman was pushing her son so hard that he'd had to invent this situation that they were in just to get the woman off his back for a few short weeks. He needed a break.

Julia couldn't imagine that she would ever have treated Marcus in such a way, if he'd have been so lucky to have reached adulthood.

The Dowager Duchess's children were a gift, and she was treating them like commodities to be shown off and sold and bred. It was all about her. What *she* wanted. What *she* needed. She was not letting her children just *be*. And Julia refused to be steamrollered by her.

'Are you all right?'

She turned at Anthony's voice and looked up at him guiltily. 'Yes. I'm sorry I caused a scene. I must go back in and apologise to Zoey.'

'You don't have to do that.'

'I do. This is her birthday dinner and I've caused a scene. With her mother, no less.'

'Probably the most excitement that's ever been experienced at one of our dining tables. I'm sure Zoey loved it. Especially you putting our mother in her place.'

'I suppose I ought to apologise to her, too.'

'Don't you dare.'

He settled onto the bench next to her. She felt soothed by his presence. His solidity. The fact that he'd come out to check on her.

'I was rude, though. I should never have told her about Marcus. Does that ruin the ruse we've created?'

'No. Absolutely not. I'll tell them I already knew about Marcus because that's the truth. All you've done is tell them the truth. We've just left *other* bits of the truth out.'

She smiled and laid a head upon his shoulder. His comfort meant a great deal to her. 'Thank you.'

'What for?'

'For being you. For not being mad at me.'

'I could never be mad at you,' he answered softly.

She turned to look at him, then. Looked up into the soft blue eyes that looked darker in the shade of the tree and the dimming light. Looked at the way the darkness of his short trimmed beard framed his jaw. Looked at his mouth. Those lips she had kissed. Lips that she knew brought both comfort and tremendous pleasure.

She wondered if she could be brave enough to kiss them again...

Could she? There was no excuse here about how she thought they ought to practise kissing in case they needed to do so in front of their families. So it looked natural. So it looked as if they'd been kissing each other that way for some time and felt comfortable doing so.

This bit was real. What she felt for him she knew was real. But how could she tell him that? His love for Yael had been complete, and there was no way she could compete with that. She was just a convenience. And he didn't want a relationship—that was why he was faking one. She'd merely agreed to help him out for a few weeks. She couldn't tell him that, for her, the rules had changed. That everything had changed.

Even though she was terrified by what she felt, something about him made her feel as if she wanted to rush headlong into whatever whirlwind of feelings and emotions she could find with him.

She knew he liked her as a friend. As a colleague at work. Knew they had a bond that could never be broken, thanks to her son. Thanks to his being the house she'd found all those years ago, in her time of need one Christmas Eve.

'I'm so glad we met again,' she said.

'Me too.'

'I never imagined when we did that we would end up here.'

'In a rose garden?' he asked jokily.

'Hiding in a rose garden because I called out your mother. Oh, my God, she's a duchess… I called out a *duchess*!'

'She needed to hear it. We've all tiptoed around her for so long. No one ever challenges her. I mean, look at what we're doing. Creating a fake relationship just so I don't have to listen to her go on and on. Maybe I should have just told her straight, so that I didn't need to drag you into my mess and make you feel this way.'

He reached up with his hand and wiped away the wetness from her cheek. She hadn't even noticed that she'd been crying.

'I needed you too. Don't forget *my* mother in all this.'

'Do you think this means we need to be firmer with our families? Tell them to butt out, because we'll live our lives our way?'

'Maybe we should…' She tried to imagine saying that to her mum. The look that would appear on her face.

They sat in silence for a moment, contemplating.

'But that would mean ending this,' he said. 'I'm not sure I'm ready to do that.'

She smiled. 'Just go back to being colleagues? Friends? I don't want that, either. Yet,' she added, feeling it was sensible to say that.

'Yet.' He nodded, agreeing. 'So, we continue?'

'We do. As agreed.'

'But the second my mother gets on the plane we go back to our own lives.'

She nodded, not trusting herself to speak as she imagined that moment. What would she do if her feelings for him continued to escalate? Would she walk away? Or would she say something?

Her gaze dropped to his mouth once more. Tempting her. The problem was, she knew how great kissing was with him. And he was so close. Right there. And they had privacy here… No one would know except them. And even if someone did see, they'd just think Anthony was consoling her. That they were having a moment.

She so very badly wanted to press her lips to his once again. To breathe into him. To lay her hand upon his chest once again and feel the rapid beating of his heart, the heat of his skin, the feel of his chest muscles beneath her touch. To feel him breathe into her as they kissed, the tickle of his beard against her skin. The taste of him...

She leaned in a little closer, daring herself to try.

Maybe if he felt the same way as her he would kiss her back, and then she would know that this thing between them went beyond their ruse. That what she'd been feeling was real because he felt it too.

All they had to do was be brave and breach that gap between them. Move from the pretend to the real...

'Found you!' said a voice.

Zoey's voice.

Julia jumped back, blushing madly, heart pounding, unsure if she could see regret in his eyes or embarrassment that she'd been about to kiss him.

Oh, God! Did I read this all wrong? Is he embarrassed for me?

'I've looked all over for you both. Are you all right?'

Julia stood up, blushing again, as if they'd been caught doing something they shouldn't. 'Zoey! Yes, I'm fine. I'm so sorry about earlier...making a scene.'

Anthony's sister waved away her apology. 'Mother had it coming. Believe me. Always acting like she's the only person in the world ever to be a mother.' She smiled, then took a step closer towards her, reaching for her hands. Holding them. 'I'm so sorry to hear about your son. Such a horrible thing for you to have gone through. If you need to talk— ever—about him, or my brother, or my mother...' She laughed. 'You call me. Any time—you hear?'

'Thank you.'

'Now, come on. We can't serve the main course until you two come back, and the chef is worried the monkfish will dry out.'

'Well, we can't have that!' Julia laughed.

'And don't worry about Mother. I've had a word with her and she won't give you a moment's more trouble. In fact, I've persuaded her not only to start on the coffee early, but also to give you an apology.'

'Oh, there's no need...'

'There's *every* need.'

As they followed Zoey back towards the house Julia risked a glance at Anthony and saw he looked quite disturbed. Confused? Surprised?

The idea that she'd been about to kiss him had clearly appalled him!

CHAPTER THIRTEEN

'YOU DON'T HAVE to walk me to my door,' Julia said later, as he dropped her back off at her flat.

'I don't mind.'

'No, honestly! It's fine.'

Julia had appeared to be quite flustered for the rest of the evening after her set-to with his mother. When they'd gone back inside the house she'd barely spoken a word to him, engaging with the other guests for most of the night. Actually, for that he'd been grateful—because there'd been a moment in the rose garden when he'd been sorely tempted to kiss her.

Not to convince anyone they were in a relationship. Just to kiss her. Because he'd wanted to. Because the urge to do so had built so strongly and so overpoweringly that he'd thought he was going mad.

They'd certainly had a moment—that was for sure. It had been nice to sit outside with her on that bench, surrounded by the scent of roses. Just talking. Just them. No pretence. Just being who they were.

There'd been a moment when she'd laid her head upon his shoulder and he'd wanted to lay his head against hers. To just be with her. To maybe reach up and stroke her face. But then she'd turned and looked up at him with such a look in her eyes... It had gone straight to his heart and something had bloomed within him. A madness. An insanity. A desire to kiss her because he wanted to, because he desired to, because he *needed* to.

He'd actually begun to lean in, because he'd thought that she'd been about to do the same thing, too. But that was crazy. Because Julia knew the parameters of this illusion, and the rules were keeping them both safe. He couldn't break them! He shouldn't step over that line.

How would she have reacted if he had? They worked together, and her job was very important to her. Her work relationship with her colleagues was incredibly important too. Was he willing to ruin that for her by overstepping the mark? She'd have said their safe word, and he'd have stopped, and then he'd have felt guilty and...

He had to get a grip on these feelings he was having for her. His future was in a direction that would require too much from her if he involved her in it. Assuming she wanted to be in it... Becoming a duchess was more than just using a title. She'd become a part of his official family history. And, despite him trying to put off his mother's wishes, she was right. He *did* need to produce an heir at some point. And Anthony did not want to put Julia through something that he knew would terrify her.

'Thank you for a lovely evening. See you at work, yes?' she asked now.

'See you tomorrow.'

He leaned in, as usual, to drop a polite, friendly, innocent kiss upon her cheek.

She smiled briefly, but it was an embarrassed smile, and she got out of the car quickly, opening her door and closing it again in seconds.

He felt a bloom of guilt wash over him. She was embarrassed for him. Embarrassed by what he'd done...trying to go in for that kiss. She had noticed. And she didn't know how to tell him to back off without hurting his feelings, no doubt.

Had he ruined this?

Had he ruined their wonderful friendship?

Anthony was furious with himself as he drove away from her place. Fuming, in fact. He'd been such a fool. Such a ridiculous romantic to let his feelings run away with him.

He'd thought this plan was perfect, but he'd never actually expected any feelings to come along with it. The connection that they would build. And now, rather stupidly, he'd started to believe that maybe this thing he had with Julia could lead to a happy-ever-after, perhaps?

Of course not. This is real life, and real life doesn't work that way.

* * *

'Thank you for meeting with me.'

Cecily Fitzpatrick, the Dowager Duchess of Weston, Anthony's mother, sat opposite Julia in the hospital cafeteria, nursing a large cappuccino as Julia sat down for her meeting with her.

Julia held her own large mug of tea, feeling nervous. She still felt awkward about her verbal bout with the Dowager, even if she had felt, at the time, that it was justified.

'No problem at all,' she said.

'How long do you have for your break?'

'Twenty minutes.'

'Right. Well, I'd best get to it, then. First of all, I wish to apologise for my remarks at Zoey's birthday dinner. One often forgets one should not take people at face value. I had no idea of your past, *your son*, and I am upset that I may have caused you distress. That was not my intention. Maybe I let the wine go to my head, making me…presumptuous.'

'You couldn't have known.'

'No, but still… I'm nervous about going to Australia and leaving Anthony alone. It troubles me. I've been trying to ensure that I leave him with someone, so that I can go without guilt. As mothers, you and I should have stood united. I'm afraid that the concern I have for my son's well-being sometimes means that I overstep and say things I should not.'

'You're a mama bear,' Julia said with a smile.

'I understand. You love him and care for him and you want to advocate for him. I remember how I felt that first day I brought my son home from the hospital. I wanted to protect him from everything. Sitting with him in that taxi, in his car seat, I was absolutely terrified and amazed at how all the other drivers drove so badly when I had my precious son in the car. And after that I spent every day just… trying to protect him from everything.'

'May I ask how…?' Cecily Fitzpatrick looked uncomfortable.

'How he died? It was SIDS. Sudden Infant Death Syndrome. I put him down at his usual bedtime, and when I woke in the morning he was gone.'

Cecily looked down and then reached for Julia's hand. 'I'm so sorry,' she said, with such feeling and empathy it brought Julia to tears. 'I can't imagine for one moment… If that had happened to Anthony or Zoey…'

The older woman blinked and wiped at her eyes, and Julia could see just how much her children meant to her.

'I don't worry so much about Zoey. She's happy. Settled. But Anthony… Well, you never stop worrying, do you? I wasn't sure that Yael was right for him in the beginning, but then he showed me how much he loved her, and how much she loved him. What she had to go through…what they *both* had to go through…broke my heart.'

'It must have been difficult.'

'It was. I did what I could, but I was helpless in the face of cancer. All I could do was hope the doctors could make it right.' She paused. 'Yael fought. She fought hard. I was so proud of her. She told me once that she wished they could have had a child before the cancer came to steal that chance away. She was upset for Anthony, you see? He really wanted children. But it never happened.' Cecily took a sip of her coffee. 'When she died, he was bereft. I thought I might lose him, too. He cut himself off from everyone…would disappear for weeks at a time. Sometimes I thought that he might do something… Well, you know.'

Julia nodded.

'But eventually he came back, and then I just wanted him to be happy. I hated seeing him alone… knowing how much being with someone would bring him happiness. And now…? Finally I can go and visit my sister without worrying about him. I can see how much he loves you. How much he cares for you. I can go, knowing that he won't be alone.'

Julia blushed and cast her head down, feeling ashamed of the lie that had been concocted for this woman who had been through so much. To worry about her son like that must have been awful. Yet this ruse was giving her peace of mind, so Julia wasn't sure exactly *how* to feel. Good or bad?

They must have been truly convincing if Cecily thought that her son loved her. But Julia knew differently. He'd been embarrassed that night in the rose garden, when she'd leaned in for a kiss. Thank goodness they'd been disturbed!

'He'll be okay. I've got him. I'll look after him for you,' she said, wanting to ensure that the Duchess, as a fellow mother, would feel some peace of mind.

She could give her that for now. Even though by the time Cecily arrived back home she would have learned that Julia had broken that promise, having split up with her son whilst she was away. What would the Dowager think of her then?

Cecily beamed, eyes gleaming. 'I know you will.' She patted Julia's hand and let out a big sigh. 'I'm glad we could have this talk. Mother to mother.'

'Yes. Me too.'

Anthony loved being in Theatre. Despite the intensity of the situation, and the laser focus of concentration that was needed, it was the place in which he felt most at home. There was something reassuring about it. The sterility, the orderliness, the beep and rhythm of the machines. The bright lights shining upon the stage that was the patient, immobilised and anaesthetised on a bed. And as for the surgery itself… From the most complicated reconstruction to the simplest fracture, he loved every procedure. They all allowed him to retreat within himself and switch off his thoughts about the world. To focus on the job in hand.

He had a full list today, and he was glad of it. Glad of the chance to not be on the ward, where

Julia would be. Glad to be free of the turmoil of his mind with regard to her. Glad of the chance to hide for a little bit without having to answer questions.

His first patient of the day was a hip replacement. Trevor Godwin, sixty-nine years of age, had always been a runner, but he had experienced pain in his left side for so long now he hadn't run for months and months, and it was making him miserable.

Anthony understood the agony of not being allowed to do the thing you wanted to do. He couldn't imagine someone telling him he couldn't operate any more. Or could never kiss Julia again.

No. Must stop thinking about her like that. We're just pretending and that will be over soon.

'Okay, everyone. Let's change a life,' he said, holding out his hand for a scalpel from his Theatre nurse, Liv.

They'd offered Trevor the option to have a spinal block and be awake during the surgery, but Trevor had requested a general anaesthetic.

Anthony made a minimal incision and then made his way down to the hip joint, to expose the full ball joint and socket. Trevor's hip was definitely in a bad way. The damage caused by advanced osteoarthritis could visibly be seen, and Anthony was glad he'd decided to perform a total hip replacement today.

'Look at that…' Liv said.

'Amazed he could still walk,' Anthony agreed as he began to remove the femoral head.

Some of the other specialists called this kind of

work carpentry. Joints. Sockets. Screws. Hammers. Some surgeons looked down on orthopaedics. But where would anyone be without a working skeleton to support the body? Without bones, people would be nothing more than gelatinous bags of skin on the floor. Anthony knew how important his work was, and how much the surgeries he performed improved lives.

'Let's prepare the bone for the insertion of the artificial hip.'

He began to remove part of the bone, shaping the interior of the femur to fit exactly the stem of the hip replacement. Once that was done, he prepared the socket in the pelvis. With the stem inserted into the thigh bone, and sealed into place with a specialised cement, the ball joint was placed on the end and fixed into the socket.

'Looks great,' Liv observed, as Anthony checked the movement of the leg, this way and that.

'Should get him back on the trails soon enough, don't you think?'

'Definitely.'

'Okay, let's close up. Pete? Can you phone through to Recovery to let them know we'll be bringing Trevor down soon? And let the ward know that I can do my next patient at about ten o clock?'

Pete was one of the Theatre technicians. 'Sure thing,' he said, and picked up the phone as Anthony began to staple the small incisions that he'd made.

Once he was done, he pulled off his gloves and

gown and reflected on a good couple of hours' worth of work.

'There are some blood and urine results waiting for you on Mrs Tucker,' Pete said, popping his head into the scrub room.

Mrs Tucker had been unknowingly suffering from a UTI when she'd come into hospital for her surgery. Thankfully it had been picked up on admission, and she'd been given some specific antibiotics to deal with the situation. No one wanted to operate when a patient's system was already stressed from fighting an infection.

'Thanks, Pete. I'm going to grab a quick bite to eat and then we'll go again.'

'Yes, boss.'

Once he'd scrubbed out, Anthony headed off to check on the blood results, expecting to use the computer to do so.

Julia was waiting by the computer terminal. He paused when he saw her, and knew she saw him pause.

She coloured and looked away as he approached.

'Morning.'

'Good morning,' she said, looking up at him and smiling. 'How are you?'

'Yeah, I'm good. Just checking on some results. You?'

'I had to bring down some notes for Dr Howard. I'm just heading back to the ward now. You're in surgery all day?'

'Yes,' he said.

'Great. I met up with your mum the other day. We had a chat.'

That was a surprise. His mother hadn't mentioned anything.

'Oh? Everything okay?'

Julia smiled. 'Yes. We talked about Marcus and then about you. About motherly worry about our sons, no matter their age.'

Well, she didn't look upset, so that was good.

'In fact, I think she saw me properly for the first time. Said she was happy to go to Australia now that she could see that you were settled with someone you...' She paused, looking uncertain.

'That I what?'

'That you love. She said that she could tell how much you loved me by the way you were looking at me.'

Was she trying to work out how badly the ruse had gone? he wondered. How far off the rails he'd gone with his feelings? Well, he would do his best to reassure her that he was bringing himself back into line.

'So our ruse is working well, then?'

She nodded quickly. Beamed a smile that went as quickly as it arrived. 'Yes.'

'Great! Well, I've got to...er...get on. I won't keep you. See you later,' he said, bending down to tap his details into the computer and access the results he needed for his next patient, dismissing her with the action.

He became aware of her hurried steps as she walked away from the station. He was groaning inwardly at how stupid he'd been to believe that she was feeling something for him. Clearly, she was not. Hopefully he had somewhat reassured her, now, that he would not embarrass them again by going in for an unwarranted, unwanted kiss.

He looked up to watch her go...felt a pang in his heart that somehow he'd screwed this up, too. He didn't want to ruin their connection. It was special between Julia and him. He'd brought her son into the world. They'd shared that magical Christmas Eve. She'd given Yael the best gift of her life. One that even he could not have given her. And for that he would be eternally grateful. He would hate himself if he screwed up their friendship.

'Julia?' he called out, before realising he was actually going to.

She turned around, a query in her gaze. 'Yes?'

He wanted to ask to meet her for coffee. He wanted to ask if he could take her out to dinner. He wanted to ask if he could dance with her, kiss her, paddle in more water with her—all of those things. But he didn't want to ruin things with her.

'Do we...er...need to go back to Paulie's soon? Do any more work on the float?' He knew there were a few little bits of construction that needed finishing. Tiny things, that clearly wouldn't need more than one of them—but, hey, no harm in asking, right? Because this wasn't for *them*…it was for the float.

'Erm… I think it's all finished.'

'Oh. Right. Okay, then.'

He smiled at her and watched her disappear through the double doors at the end of the corridor. Then cursed silently as he punched in his password to bring up the urinalysis and blood results. The infection had been cleared and Mrs Tucker was ready for the arthroscopic surgery on her knee.

He double-checked the details, just in case. He didn't want his frustration to result in any silly mistakes.

A doctor slumped into a chair next to him. Dr Howard—a young registrar with a bit of a reputation for dating the nurses.

'Hey, do you know her?' he asked.

'Who?' Anthony was distracted.

'That nurse you were talking to. Joanne? Julianne?'

'Julia.' He was annoyed that Dr Howard couldn't even get her name right. 'Yes. Why?'

'She's cute… Know if she's single?'

And even though he knew he ought to give Julia the opportunity to make her own mind up about people, the opportunity to find a real relationship, he couldn't help but steer her away from this guy.

'No, she's involved with someone.'

Technically, he reasoned, it was true.

'Oh. Shame. She's hot.'

Anthony gave him a withering stare.

CHAPTER FOURTEEN

I'M DOING IT AGAIN, Julia thought. I'm falling in love with an unavailable man.

Her own father had never been emotionally available. Jake, Marcus's father, had not been available at all, and had left her to deal with their child's death alone. And now she could feel herself pining for a guy who was in a fake relationship with her and who would dump her the moment his mother boarded an aeroplane.

He would do it nicely. It wouldn't be like the break-up with Jake. Knowing Anthony, he would be kind, gracious…maybe buy her some flowers, drop a kiss onto her cheek and wish her the best. But then it would all be over and she would have to watch him walk away.

They would just be friends after that. Because he wasn't ready. He'd told her that right at the beginning.

Just like I told him the same thing.

But her feelings had changed the more she'd got to know him. The more she'd got to experience his life. The more he'd shared hers. Her mother adored him, her friends loved him and so did she.

Was she ready to deal with yet another broken heart? Or should she try to be brave enough to tell him that her feelings had changed?

How can I? If he is where I think he is, he's going to turn me down—and then work will be awkward.

Look at how their conversation had gone when she'd repeated to him his mother's words about the way Anthony looked at her. Told him that Cecily had said she could tell he loved her. What had he answered with?

'So the ruse is working, then?'

Like a dagger to her heart.

More than anything, she didn't want that feeling. She wanted to keep Anthony's friendship, the connection they had. So maybe, instead of being awkward with him and uncomfortable since that near-kiss, she ought to be friendly and return to the parameters that they had set earlier, to keep each other safe?

Unable to find him on the ward, she texted him, asking for a minute to talk to him. When he arrived, still in his scrubs, tired from a long day in surgery, she hurried to his side with a beaming smile.

'Can I talk to you about Mrs Tucker, Mr Fitzpatrick?' she asked, in a tone that should imply to anyone listening that their chat was work-related.

'Is there a problem?'

She guided him over to one side of the room.

'Mrs Tucker is absolutely fine. I just wanted to talk to you.'

'Oh. Okay.'

'You asked about working on the float?'

'Mm-hmm.' He smiled at a nurse who passed by, holding refills for the glove boxes at the nurses' station.

'We could go out and do something else, if you wanted?'

'Like what?'

She shrugged. 'I don't know… But until your mother goes away I think we ought to be seen still doing things that suggest we're in a relationship. What about going for coffee? Or maybe dinner? Somewhere we might be seen by your family or mine?'

He smiled and nodded. 'Sure. When?'

'Your mother leaves in a couple of days…which means we don't have much time left together. Maybe we could go out and celebrate a…a job well done?'

'Well, actually, my second cousin Tobias is having a dinner dance thing at his place the night before my mother leaves. We could attend that?'

It sounded perfect. One last hurrah with him that she could treasure for ever. Because she didn't want to end things on bad terms. She wanted to remember this time fondly.

'Do I have to get another dress?'

'Probably. But I can reimburse you for any expenses.'

She smiled. 'No need. This one's on me.' She looked about them…saw the nurse with the gloves looking at them. 'I'll get to that right away, Mr Fitzpatrick. Thank you,' she said loudly as she walked away from him, nodding at the nurse with a smile as she passed.

She felt better.

She'd made things right.

Even if it was going to break her heart.

He texted her with more details later, and she sent him pictures of possible dresses and asked which he thought might suit her best.

Anthony thought she would look beautiful in any of them, but refrained from saying so, instead stating they were all lovely. She sent back a reply saying that she would surprise him, then.

The fact that her awkwardness with him had gone gladdened him immensely. He'd not been able to bear the disruption between them, and because of that he knew he had to harden his heart immediately. He'd let his emotions run away with him. Had let his hopes grow when reality was showing him that he needed to rein them in.

And so, when the night arrived for Tobias's dinner dance, he put back up all the walls that had surrounded him since Yael's passing, knowing that he needed to do so in order to cope with the moment when the illusion ended and he and Julia would shake hands and part as friends.

He stood on her doorstep, waiting for her to answer the door, taking deep breaths, hardening his heart. He was ready for the reveal, determined to be polite, to compliment her and say she looked beautiful, but to do so in a way that was detached. Polite. Non-committal.

He heard her footsteps and got a flashback to the dress she'd worn at his mother's charity ball. That blush-pink number that she'd looked so stunning in. No dress was going to be better than that, surely?

But when she opened the door and revealed herself wearing a body-hugging dark purple silk number, which hugged her in all the right places, he had to fight to stop his jaw from hitting the ground.

'Wow! You look...amazing.'

'Is it all right?' she asked, turning so that he could view it from all angles.

He loved the way the silk curved over her backside...how most of her back was exposed, revealing an expanse of tempting flesh...how her legs seemed to go on for days through the split that began at mid-thigh. He saw the glint of an ankle bracelet...her painted toes peeking from matching high heeled shoes. The urge to reach out, to touch, to glide his fingers up the length of her legs, trace her spine, her neck, her lips, was just *overwhelming*.

Instead he stepped back, creating more space

between them, and produced the politest smile he could, nodding. 'It's perfect.'

'Great. I wasn't sure.'

He opened the car door for her. No chauffeur tonight. He made himself look away as she settled into the seat and then swung those endless legs inside the vehicle, smoothing her skirt and placing her small clutch bag on her lap. Once she was in, he closed the door and walked round to his own side, giving himself a pep talk, telling himself he could do this. It was just Julia. His friend, his colleague.

But his brain wanted to tell him so many other things. She wasn't '*just* Julia'. She was the woman he had come to care for greatly. The woman he would go to the ends of the earth to protect. The woman who had brought happiness back into his life. Wonder. Joy. The ability to laugh again and not feel guilty. The woman he thought about constantly. The woman he knew Yael would have loved, too.

The woman he *desired*.

But he could not have her. She had made that plain. She had told him she wasn't ready for a relationship. Had looked embarrassed when he'd leaned in for that kiss—had been so uncomfortable with him that they had avoided each other for a little while and he'd hated that.

As he drove towards Tobias's house he tried to act relaxed. Nonchalant. But his body was thrilled by the proximity of her. By her perfume in the small, intimate space of the car. In his peripheral vision his gaze caught glimpses of diamante in the dress he hadn't noticed before, glittering in the moonlight. Caught the way the dress shaped her delicious curves. A hint of cleavage. His physical attraction to her was threatening to burst forth from behind walls that already had huge cracks in them.

'One last hurrah,' she said.

'Mm…' he said, not trusting himself to speak yet.

Part of him wanted this night to go on for ever. For it never to end. But he knew that time would go by in an instant. At some point he would drive her home and say goodbye and that would be the end of their ruse. Their illusion. He would take his mother to the airport tomorrow and wave her off, knowing he was alone even if his mother thought differently. He would wait for her return in a couple of months before letting her know that he and Julia had not worked out.

And somehow he would have to see her at work every day and deal with that.

'I've had a great time doing this—just so you know,' she said. 'It's actually been fun. Almost a life-swap. Like you see on those shows on television.'

He smiled and glanced at her briefly, torturing himself with her beauty.

'I guess I just want to say thank you, too,' she went on. 'It's been nice not having people going on at me about finding someone to be with.'

'Me too.'

It had been nice. But what had been nicer were the conversations he'd had with people who had met Julia. Zoey. His mother. His friends. All of them telling him how they made such a great couple. How they were so perfectly suited.

Soul mates.

In the beginning, he'd simply smiled and nodded, pleased that they had managed to convince entire swathes of people that they were in a real relationship, but now that he was deeper into it he hated that he couldn't have it for real.

What would they all say when he declared it was over? Would he have to deal with their pity? Their sympathy? Their disbelief?

Maybe I should go away for a bit? Go travelling, or something, to avoid all that?

'It's going to be strange when it's over,' she mused.

'It is,' he replied. 'I was just thinking that I might go away for a bit afterwards. You know…to avoid the pity party when people find out that we're not together any more.'

'Great idea. I might do the same thing.'

'Maybe stagger our vacations, though. Make sure people don't think we're together.'

'Where would you go?'

He shrugged. 'Not sure. Lake Garda? Cannes?'

'Wow. Okay… I was thinking about Scotland.'

'You like Scotland?'

'I've never been. But there are so many places

that look interesting and beautiful up there. I've always wanted to go.'

He'd been to Scotland and she was right. There was the beauty of Loch Lomond. The historical city of Edinburgh. The amazing Isle of Skye. Glencoe. Iona. Orkney. He could imagine taking her to all those places. Watching her eyes brighten with delight as she visited them. Holding her hand as they walked. Maybe paddling with her in Loch Ness...

'I can recommend a few places for you,' he said.

'Great.'

They were quiet as he pulled to a stop outside Tobias's place. He walked around the car to open her door and held out his hand, gazing at her with adoration as she alighted from the vehicle and adjusted her dress.

He felt so lucky that she had come into his life—even if it had been just for such a short while. He would remember his time with her fondly. Never forget.

He could hear music playing as they neared the house. They were presented with drinks as they entered. He saw faces he knew, and faces he didn't, and they were soon met by members of his family. He introduced Julia to those who had never met her before, and said hello to those who had.

Tobias clapped him on the back and gave him a huge hug, before turning to Julia, taking her hand and kissing the back of it. 'Nice to meet you at last, Julia. I've heard all about you!' he said.

'Nice to meet you, too. You have a beautiful home.'

'This old thing? Needs redecorating, but it'll do.'

He was being self-deprecating. Anthony knew Tobias had taken on this old house about eight years ago, renovating and restoring it to its former grandeur. He was an architect, and it had become a passion project. Anthony knew how much work and investment had gone into it, despite the way Tobias was playing it down.

'Well, I think it's lovely,' said Julia.

'And so are you. Do you mind if I have this dance?'

Tobias held out his hand towards Julia. She glanced at Anthony before turning back to his cousin.

'Of course.'

Anthony didn't examine his feelings too closely as he watched Julia being led onto the dance floor by Tobias. He felt a little bit of everything. Envy. Loss. Reluctance. But most of all he found himself sneaking the opportunity to just look at her whilst she moved across the floor in Tobias's arms.

This is what it will be like, he thought. *When she finds someone else.*

She was smiling at his cousin. Laughing at something Tobias was saying. Tobias was a funny guy, quite the charmer, and he had always been successful with the ladies before settling down with his sweetheart. Anthony wondered where Tobias's wife was. What she thought of her husband dancing with Julia.

Probably nothing at all. I'm just feeling jealous.

Julia's eyes gleamed, her smile was broad, and the way that dress skimmed her body, accentuating all those sumptuous curves and softness, made his heart pound.

But she was not to be his.

And no doubt she would be glad when this was over.

He accepted another drink from a passing member of staff.

When the music finished, Tobias escorted Julia back to him. 'Your turn, I think.'

'Thank you. I was wondering when I'd get to dance with the lady *I* brought to the party.'

Tobias mouthed a word at him. *Stunning.* Then slipped away to attend to his other guests.

Julia turned to look at Anthony. 'He's quite a character.'

'Mm… He is.'

'Wicked sense of humour!'

'Yes, he has. I hope he wasn't too rude?'

'Far from it.'

'Would you like a drink?'

She looked up at him. 'No, I want to dance. I want us to dance the night away. Make it memorable, seeing as this is our last time.'

Did she look sad?

No. It was his own wishful thinking. It had to be.

And she was right. This would be their last night together. There was no reason for them to spend their leisure hours with each other ever again.

He took her hand and led her back to the dance floor as a slow and dreamy number began to play. They'd begun this at a dance. It seemed only fitting that it should end this way, too.

He tried to keep his thoughts and his feelings straight as he pulled her close, but the way she was looking into his eyes as they began to move was making that extremely difficult.

'Are you looking forward to your mother going away?' she asked.

'I'm happy that she's going to get away for a bit. She hasn't had a break in years—so, yes, it will be good for her.'

'What are you going to do whilst she's away?'

'I haven't really thought about it. Maybe just chill. Read.' He met her gaze. 'When are you going to tell your family that we've split up?'

She looked away, eyeing the other couples on the dance floor. 'I don't know. Maybe in a few weeks?'

He nodded. 'Will they be okay with it?'

'They'll be disappointed… But hopefully they'll be pleased that I've dipped my toes back into the dating waters.'

He smiled, remembering those times she'd taken him paddling. The water fountain. The river. The delight it had given her.

'You've made me dip my toes into water, too.'

She smiled shyly back at him. 'We had fun, didn't we?'

'We did.'

'We made a pretty convincing couple.'

He sighed. 'Yes.'

'Did you ever...?' She stopped and blushed.

'What?'

'Did you ever think what it might be like for real?'

His heart almost leapt from his chest. Could she feel it pounding through his jacket? Could she see his pulse thrumming in his throat? Feel the soaring of his temperature?

The urge to tell her the truth overwhelmed him. This way he could actually explain how he'd been feeling! 'Of course I thought about it!'

But then his throat closed up as her eyes widened and he hurried to say more, looking away from her. It was the only way he could gather. Regroup.

'What we were doing lent itself to those kinds of thoughts,' he said. 'But... I never took it seriously,' he lied.

She nodded. 'No, nor me,' she said quietly.

He continued to lead her around the dance floor, unable to look her in the eyes. If this relationship had been real, they would never have made it away from her flat once he'd seen her in that dress. He'd have taken her hand and raised it above her head. Made her give him a turn. And then he would have begun kissing her. And they'd have gone back inside. And then he would have helped her remove it...

I can't keep thinking like this!

But he couldn't stop the thoughts. They bombarded him.

If they'd been in a real relationship he would have looked at the split in her dress in the car and he would have placed a hand upon her knee as he drove, unable to not touch her. He would not have let Tobias dance with her. He would have held on to her and maybe found an empty room somewhere, where he would have kissed her like she'd never been kissed before. Perhaps he would have been dancing with her like he was dancing with her now, but he would be looking deep into her eyes and telling her silently of all the things he wanted to do with her when he got her home.

But most of all he would have been enjoying his time with her guilt-free. He wouldn't be hiding his real feelings from her. She would know them. He would be able to tell her how much she meant to him. Sit with her on her couch and watch trashy television. Make her tea. Treat her like a queen. Wake up with her every morning and thank the heavens that his life was so blessed after he'd begun to believe that it could never be blessed again.

The bombardment of his feelings left him feeling dizzy.

'Excuse me a moment,' he said, letting her go and walking off the dance floor to find a bathroom.

He needed to splash some water on his face and regain some sort of bloody control.

Julia felt bewildered when Anthony suddenly left her in the middle of the dance floor. Had she said something wrong? She didn't think so. All she'd done was agree with what he'd said, even though it had been painful to lie.

Of course she'd had thoughts about them being a couple for real.

But she'd never thought that in creating this ruse for others she would have to lie to *him*, too.

How had it got so complicated?

The sooner I'm out of this mess, the better!

Embarrassed, and hoping no one had noticed, she headed over to the side of the room, to hide amongst the assembled guests. But no sooner had she arrived than someone was touching her arm.

'Julia!'

She turned. Cecily Fitzpatrick. Anthony's mother.

'Cecily! How are you?'

'I'm fine. Is Anthony all right? I saw him leave you just now. He looked…ill, or something.'

Julia knew she couldn't muck up the plan now. Not when they were so close to the end. The whole point of this was so that his mother could fly away like a little bird and not worry about her son for two months whilst she enjoyed Adelaide with her sister.

'He was a little hot. I think he said he was going to splash some water on his face,' she said, hoping it sounded convincing.

'Yes, it is warm in here, isn't it? That dress you're wearing is divine!'

'Oh, this? Thank you.' She didn't want to say that she'd actually got it for a very reasonable price from a high street store. 'Are you excited for tomorrow?' she asked.

'Absolutely! I haven't seen Amelia for ages, and it will be nice to catch up with all my nieces and nephews over there. Do you know, my sister became a grandparent for the fourth time last month?'

'No, I hadn't heard that.'

'I can't wait to hold the little one. You don't mind me talking about babies?'

'Of course not! They're a joy.'

Cecily beamed. 'I knew you'd understand. And one day, I'm sure, you'll hold another one of your own. Maybe Anthony's! I know that he'll make a wonderful father.'

Julia believed her. 'I'm sure he will.'

'You know, when I get back you and I should meet up. Go out for dinner together, or something. Perhaps with Zoey. Just us girls.'

'That would be lovely,' she said, knowing it would never happen.

She would never be one of *'us girls'*. She wasn't now. It was all just pretend. It was as if she'd been in a dressing up box and was now playing a role. Anthony's girlfriend.

It would have been a nice romantic story for her and Anthony to have fallen in love for real, though. She could picture it so easily… And she loved everyone that she'd met in his world. They were not pretentious, and they all had Anthony's best interests at heart. They loved him.

And so do I.

'I'll ring you when I get back,' said his mother. 'Oh, there's Jasmine! I simply must go and talk to her about her interior designer… Excuse me.'

And then Cecily was gone. Like a force of nature. Cutting a swathe through the guests to arrive at the side of a middle-aged woman in a red dress.

Julia watched them embrace and drop air kisses either side of each other's cheeks.

'Sorry about that.'

She turned. Anthony was back, looking a lot more composed than earlier. Maybe he really had gone to splash water on his face.

'Everything all right?' she asked.

'Absolutely. I saw you talking to Mother.'

'She wants us to meet up when she gets back from Australia.'

'Oh. You didn't say anything?'

'Of course not!'

'Good. The quicker this is all over, the better.'

CHAPTER FIFTEEN

'THE QUICKER THIS is all over, the better.'

Anthony had driven her home and now he sat in the driver's seat, not really looking at her. He'd been strange all evening, and she wondered if someone had said something to him that had upset him.

'Are you all right?' she asked.

'I'm fine.'

'You've been weird all night.'

'Have I?'

'Yes, you have. I thought tonight would be...joyful. That we'd both be thrilled with our success. But you don't seem to be.'

The quicker this is over, the better.

She was trying her best not to let his words rend her heart in two, but it was difficult.

Anthony bit his lip before speaking. 'I am thrilled. Of course I am. And I'm very grateful that you've done all that for me.'

'But...?'

He looked as if he was going to say something else. She hoped that he would. That he would say something along the lines of *I've made a mistake. I don't want this to be a lie. I want this thing between us to be real.*

But he didn't. Of course he didn't. That was just her allowing her romantic illusions to break through her logical reasoning. Things like that didn't happen to her. Julia Morris was not a woman who ever got a happy ending. She was doomed to live her life on the edge of disappointment, let-downs and broken hearts.

This situation was no different. No matter how much she wanted it to be otherwise.

'But nothing,' he said. 'I'm not sure what you want me to say.'

'I want you to say…' she began, her voice raised. But then she was stopping herself. Because if she begged him to tell her that he wanted this to be real and he laughed at her, or said something that broke her heart for real…

Julia didn't need to hear him actually *say* it. Tell her that they couldn't be anything more than friends. Because that would truly break her heart. So it was easier not to push for it.

'I want you to say that we've had a good time and that it was fun. And for you to sound like you mean it. Not be in this…this weird mood you're in. It can't end with this mood. I know you want all this to be over now, but could you at least sound like you had a good time?'

Anthony looked down for a moment, then turned

in his seat to look at her, his eyes gleaming in the dark shadows of the car's interior. 'I've had an amazing time with you. Like I could never have imagined. It's been the most fun I've had in years,' he said, reaching for her hand and squeezing it.

And...?

'That's it?' she demanded.

She yearned for him to say more, but he remained quiet. Just sat there, holding her hand. And even though she longed to stay like that for ever, she knew she had to end this. He was never going to say what she truly wanted him to say, and she was too scared to say it herself. So instead she just raised his hand to her lips, kissed the back of it and whispered goodbye, alighting from the car and walking to her door without looking back. Because she knew that if she did it would break her heart.

Unlocking the door, she slipped inside and closed it behind her, tears stinging her eyes as she heard his car drive away. The realisation that it was all over was just too much for her damaged and fragile heart to handle.

Anthony stayed at the airport long enough to watch his mother's flight take off. He stood there for a long while, watching the aeroplane disappear into the distance, hearing his mother's last words repeated over and over again in his mind.

'You look after Julia, do you hear? She's everything.'

She was everything.

He hated it that his mother was right, but what could he do? He wasn't able to admit out loud that Julia had brought him more happiness in the last few weeks than he'd ever thought possible and it was now over. They had to go back to just being work colleagues. It didn't sit well with him at all.

All of last night he'd lain awake, his brain presenting him conflicting images and emotions. Tobias taking Julia's hand and leading her onto the dance floor. Dr Howard ogling Julia in the hospital and asking him if he knew if she was single. One day that would be real...her being with someone else.

It felt wrong.

But there were other, happier memories. Seeing her in that dress she'd worn for his mother's charity ball. Listening to her laugh as she painted wood for the float, a smear of paint across her cheek. Watching the delight on her face as she encouraged him to paddle with her in the river. The jacket potato stall in the square. Twirling around the dance floor with her in a waltz. Seeing the way she'd looked into his eyes. The way she'd looked at him as she'd laughed at his jokes. The way she'd held his hand and how that had made him feel.

Those practice kisses...

They'd been so convincing, his mother had questioned him on the way to the airport. She'd asked if their relationship was serious. If he could imagine himself popping the question to her one day.

He'd made non-committal noises. Changed the subject. But now he thought about those questions. Questions he'd never allowed himself to think about before.

Because he *could* imagine it. He'd dreamed about her saying yes to him. And now he'd left her in such a way she could say yes to someone else—because he was too damned afraid of her saying no to him.

And if she says no…? Yes, it'll hurt like hell. And we'll have to find a way to carry on working together so that it isn't awkward. I could check the rota. Stay more in Theatre. Get my registrars to do the rounds and report back.

But he knew he would never do that. That wasn't the kind of doctor he was. He was hands on. He was involved. He liked to reassure patients himself, if he was the one doing their surgery, and he liked to check on them afterwards. Answer their questions as only their surgeon could.

He and Julia were both adults. They would find a way to put it all behind them for the sake of their jobs.

But what if she didn't say no…?

If those kisses were real…?

If she wanted more but was also afraid to say it…?

Hadn't she asked him often enough? Hadn't she

given him ample opportunity to say something? Perhaps tell the truth?

Anthony looked up at the sky, at the clouds his mother's plane had disappeared into. Had he missed all the clues? Had he been so afraid of rejection he'd missed the subtle signs she'd been giving him? Imagine if he had... What if he didn't have to continue the ruse with his mother because he and Julia really were going out with each other?

Then those kisses would be *real*!

He glanced at his watch. He knew where she would be. It was the float parade that afternoon. She was going to watch it. Cheer her friends on. Rattle a bucket.

He could meet her there!

Or am I being totally crazy?

Julia so wanted to enjoy the float parade. So she pushed her heartbreak to one side and forced a smile onto her face as the floats passed, trying her damnedest not to think about all those hours spent with Anthony, helping make the float with Paulie, Yvette and Janine.

She could see their float coming. Janine was driving the truck and Paulie and some of the others were dressed up in superhero outfits. Yvette was dressed as a princess. She could see them waving at the crowds, as a band played pop music on a float nearby, blasting the sound from speakers.

The crowds were loving the parade, waving banners, holding balloons. Kids sat on the shoulders of their parents as they waved and licked ice creams. She imagined what it would have been like to stand here with Marcus. He would have loved this. At least she hoped so...

But as her friends' float got closer she could see another figure standing in the castle with them. Somebody dressed as a knight in full armour.

Whoever he is, he must be hot.

Odd, though, that none of her friends had mentioned there was going to be a knight on the float. Perhaps it wasn't anyone she knew?

But she waved anyway as the float grew closer, beaming a smile, showing her support and her joy to her friends, even though inside she felt so sad she'd almost not come.

I promised, though.

And she'd also had wanted to see the full effect of the castle after all those hours of work.

Janine waved at her from behind the wheel, then stopped the float in front of her.

What are you doing? Julia mouthed to her friend, not sure what was going on.

As she watched, Paulie and Yvette blew her kisses. And then the knight, in his armour, descended the steps at the back of the faux castle and got off the float.

Janine began driving again, waving goodbye, and Julia frowned in confusion. The knight was coming towards her, his armour actually clanking, a sword at his hip, sheathed in a scabbard.

What is this?

There was something familiar about him… but she couldn't think too hard about it because the knight was reaching behind his breastplate for something and when he removed his gauntleted hand, he held a piece of pink silk and proffered it to her.

All around her, the crowd was clapping and cheering. Julia took the kerchief, remembering where she'd seen in films knights offering their tokens to princesses before they went into battle.

And then the knight reached up to his helmet and removed it. And before she knew it she was looking at Anthony. It was *him*. It was *his* suit of armour that she'd recognised. The one that had been at his house.

'What are you doing?' she asked, laughing, so pleased to see him she'd forgotten all her woes. Their parting. Her heartbreak.

'My lady.' He gave a bow. 'Julia… As a man, I was not brave enough to ask for your hand. But as a knight of the realm…' he smiled as he patted his chest '…and with my heart protected by armour plating, I ask you for it now.'

'Anthony!'

Was this a joke? More of the role-playing they'd been doing?

'You are my heart. You have become my everything. I ask that you consider becoming my lady for life. Fear not saying no. I will survive it. But know ye that if you say yes, then I will spend every day of the rest of my life being proud that you are my lady and proclaiming our happiness to the world. What say you?'

Julia half gasped, half laughed at the incredulity of the moment. 'Are you asking me to be your girlfriend?'

'No. I'm asking you to be my *wife*.'

She needed someone to pinch her. Was this truly happening? Was this really Anthony? Being her knight in shining armour? This was crazy!

But it was also everything she'd ever wanted. For she could see a future with him. Had dreamed of a future with him. And she would accept his love, his ring, without a second of doubt.

She took his hand in hers. 'I accept.'

Around them, the assembled crowd went crazy as Anthony scooped her up and twirled her around before kissing her.

One kiss. Two. Three. She didn't want it to stop.

Real kisses. Not pretend. And she felt his love in every one of them.

Becoming his duchess would be far better than becoming his lady.

EPILOGUE

'I CAN'T BELIEVE it ended like that!' Julia cried, reaching for a tissue from the box and dabbing at her eyes as the final credits rolled on the movie she and Anthony had been watching at home.

'Are you crying because of the happy ending, or crying because of the baby?' Anthony asked, smiling at his wife where she sat on the couch, her feet on a footstool, because she'd learned that it helped with her swollen ankles towards the end of the day.

Julia was at full term and their baby would come any day now. They were both so excited, and they had no idea what they were having as they wanted it to be a surprise.

'I don't know! Both!' she said, hiccupping a laugh as she dabbed at her tears and rubbed her belly at the same time.

'Baby kicking?' he asked.

'No. I feel crampy.'

'Labour crampy?' he asked, sitting forward.

Technically, she was two days past her due date. She had an appointment in three days' time to see the midwife and have a sweep of her membranes done, if she wanted to.

She looked at him, suddenly nervous. 'Maybe? I don't know.'

He understood. He knew she was anxious about having this baby, and they'd waited a long time before deciding to try for a child. He'd wanted Julia to be ready. Not to feel forced into doing something that he knew terrified her. But they'd spoken to lots of doctors. Lots of specialists. And they'd had counselling. They'd been reassured, also, by buying lots of equipment. Video monitors. Oxygen monitors. They were both medically trained and they would do absolutely everything they could to avoid anything bad happening.

Julia had not wanted to live in fear.

'I nearly lost you because I was afraid,' she'd told him in those early days. *'And now look at how happy we are. If I can be brave enough to try again, imagine how happy we would be!'*

And they were. Extremely happy. Happier than any two people had a right to be.

They'd come clean to both their families. Told them about the ruse. Everyone thought it was a cool story, thankfully. Something to tell their children. And their grandchildren, one day.

Most people at work had not been surprised. And Rosaria hadn't even said anything mean. She'd just chuckled and said, with a big smile, *'I knew something was going on!'*

Julia got up and began walking off the cramp. He walked with her, holding her hand.

'How long did that one last?' he asked.

'Only about thirty seconds. Not long.'

'I guess we wait to see if you have another?'

'Yes.' She nodded, stopping, turning to look up into his eyes. 'I love you.'

'I love you, too. Both of you,' he said, laying a hand on her bump, feeling her skin tighten beneath his fingertips. 'Is that another? Already?'

She laughed. 'Yes!'

The contractions began to come thick and fast. They paced. They sat. They paced some more. And when her waters broke they phoned the hospital and made their way in.

It felt strange to be going into a hospital as patients and family, rather than as doctor and nurse, but the midwives there made them feel they were special, and they'd organised a private room for Julia to labour in.

She was monitored, briefly, to check her contractions and monitor the baby's heart, and they joked with each other about what the birth weight might be.

'About seven pounds?' Julia guessed.

'I'm thinking more like nine pounds,' said Anthony. 'I was a big baby.'

'You still are,' she joked—before another contraction hit and she had to breathe her way through it.

He held her hand. He coached her. Stroked her

when she asked for it. Dabbed her forehead with a cold, wet flannel when she needed it. And before they knew it she was fully dilated.

'I'm scared,' she said, reaching for his hand.

He kissed her, pressed his forehead to hers and looked deep into her eyes. 'I know. But we can do this, you and I. We're in this together. And, actually, you're the bravest woman I've ever known.'

'But what if…?' She couldn't finish her sentence, and her eyes filled with tears.

He reached into his pocket, pulled out his phone and brought up the photo she'd shared with him of Marcus, smiling into the camera. 'He's going to look after us. He never left you. He's in there.' He gestured at her chest. 'In your heart and mine. And no matter what, he always will be.'

She nodded. It was what she needed to hear as she began to push.

Anthony watched the woman he loved and adored battle her way through the intense contractions, pushing hard, breathing heavily. The look of determination on her face never faltered. Never wavered.

She was a mother.

She had never stopped being a mother.

And now she was going to make them a family.

* * * * *

If you enjoyed this story,
check out these other great reads from
Louisa Heaton

Finding a Family Next Door
Best Friend to Husband?
Resisting the Single Dad Surgeon
A Mistletoe Marriage Reunion

All available now!